TALES & LEGENDS OF INDIA

TALES & LEGENDS OF INDIA

Elaine King

New Editions Publishing House

New Editions Publishing House
64-A, Adhchini, Sri Aurobindo Marg,
New Delhi 110-017

Published in 1998 by
New Editions Publishing House
Reprinted 2000

ISBN 81-7716-000-1

Rs. 145.00
Typeset in Bookman
Illustrations: Kumar Ramesh
Cover and Book Design
Art Creations
45, Nehru Apartments, Kalkaji, New Delhi

Printed and bound in India by
Saurabh Print-O-Pack, Noida

Contents

INTRODUCTION

Indian legends today embody the historical traditions of the usually illiterate mass of the people. They belong neither to the great literary epics such as the *Mahabharata* and the *Ramayana*, nor to the folk tale, whether amusing or didactic, because they are based on historical personages and they are kept alive, and to some extent modified to suit the times, by the bards. Nevertheless bardic tradition often uses material which originated as a folk story, was then incorporated into literary works as part of their discursive embellishment, and then passed back into the common folk currency. It incorporates fairy-tale elements, but Indian fairytales are often based on historical fact, as are Western epics, fairytales and nursery rhymes.

Mogul rule brought a radical change to these legends. The bards who handed them down from generation to generation and recited or sang them in public had been honoured figures in pre-Mogul India. But Moslem iconoclasm frowned on many legendary motifs, and the bards tended to sink in caste; their legends were relegated from the princely court to the women's apartments or to the market place. One result, as will be observed, is a strong element of caste in many of the legends. The conflict of Hinduism and Islam also figures prominently.

In the same way the individual bard often suits his

fancy as to which of various devices he will use to move his story along. Among such stock motifs represented in these legends we can recognize the hero's miraculous birth following many year's effort to overcome the lack of an heir, the pregnancy possibly due to the mother eating a magic seed; the wicked stepmother or co-wife, historically based on rajas' habits of marrying throughout life for political reasons; the hero setting out in the world with a friend, especially a minister or his son; the prophetic dream; overhearing speaking animals; helping animals and being rewarded by them; the snake in its ambiguous role, part earth godling and guardian of precious stones, and part demon; the supernatural selection or origin of a bride, which may justify a dynastic change; or the princess who marries the person who cures her illness. Allied to this are the ordeals: the impossible tasks; the gambling match; the swayamvara; conflict with rakshasas. Often these incidents assume greater importance than the basic story; the imaginative way in which they are used and interwoven is the distinguishing mark of a great bard's art.

Tales from Eastern India

The Jackal-mad

The following legend from Assam relates to the troubled succession to kingdom of the great Vikramaditya. The folk tale element of the story is perhaps intensified by the great distance from Assam of Vikramaditya's capital of Ujjain, in the northern Deccan, and still more of the kingdom of Bhuj, which is further west, in Kutch. The motif of the prince with the animal skin occurs in many Bengali tales. Usually he is the son of the youngest of seven ranis who are each given a magic fruit which enables them to become pregnant. The senior wives allow the seventh's fruit to be spoiled by some animal, so that the youngest rani gives birth to a son whose skin is that the animal: monkey, dog, caterpillar, etc. The son nevertheless marries a beautiful princess, who redeems her husband by burning the skin, which he has temporarily shed.

When the great king Vikramaditya began to feel that his death was near, his son and daughter-in-law, the daughter of the king of Bhuj, took his bed to the distant banks of the Ganges, where Vikramaditya piously prepared to meet death. The king, rallying one day, felt a wish to smoke his gold hookah. While the son ran to fetch it, the king, unaware of his absence, explained that all the kingdom's wealth was hidden: a hundred thousand rupees under the palace bath stone; and as much again buried under Vikramaditya's bed. In order to obtain this money all his son had to do was to take his basil-wood rosary in his hand and say: 'Reveal yourself, wealth of my father.' Having said this, Vikramaditya died. His daughter-in-law had carefully noted his instructions, but when her husband returned with the hookah, she told him that there had been no last message.

Ali Ujjain began a life of poverty verging on destitution, Vikramaditya's son was king in name only; so poor was he that he had to go work, and even to beg. He was careful, however, always to divide his money equally into three — a third for his wife, a third for his mother and a third for himself — so his wife might have no cause for complaint.

One day, while the son was out working, a message came from the king of Bhuj inviting his daughter and son-in-law to a banquet and requesting his daughter to help entertain the guests. She quickly left for her father's palace, asking her mother-in-law to urge her son to follow and to be sure to sit by the central pillar of the banqueting hall so that his wife would not miss him. But when her husband arrived she totally ignored him; and when he asked her for food, she flew into a rage and, leaving the guests unattended, retired to the house of anger, the room in a palace to which a lady would withdraw when she wished to express great displeasure. When her father asked what troubled her, she told him that the guest sitting near the central pillar had insulted her and that she would not leave the house of anger till she had seen his blood. The king

therefore ordered the execution of the guest; but his ministers, who thought the princess's whim unjust, bribed the executioner to kill a dog and show the princess its blood. The princes, appeased, reappeared among the guests and the banquet proceeded. Her husband, meanwhile, was hidden in the palace sweeper's hut.

Now unknown to anyone else in the palace, this low-caste sweeper was the lover of the infamous princess; and that night, as soon as the guests had departed, she came to visit him in his hut. From his hiding place her husband in horror recognized her voice as she exulted at having finally rid herself of him and at having preserved the secret of Vikramaditya's wealth, on which she and her lover would be able to live in luxury the rest of their lives; and then she told the sweeper the formula for calling forth the three hundred thousand rupees. As soon as they were asleep her husband slipped out of the hut, returned home, and called forth the money. Then he gave part of it to his mother and buried the rest in a lake.

Fearing danger if he exposed himself to his wife's vengeance, he disguised his features with a mask made of a jackal's head and he draped the jackal's skin about him. Thus he wandered about from village to village, everywhere earning the nickname 'Jackal-mad'. Eventually he reached another kingdom, where he went to a goldsmith who was making royal jewelry and persuaded him to sell it to him by offering double the price. Then he put the jewellery on beneath his jackal skin, smeared himself with sticky syrup so that flies swarmed all over him and went to lie on a path near the palace, where he had discovered that the king's daughter and her friend, a nobleman's daughter, used to walk every morning.

Every day he would lie across their path and the nobleman's daughter would abuse him and order him to move. One day, however, the Jackal-mad refused to move unless the princess would promise to come back; otherwise she would have to jump

over him. After some reflection, the princess agreed, saying that she promised three times to come to him (the binding triple oath of Moslem usage), and the Jackal-mad allowed her to pass.

As soon as she reached her father's palace the princess retired to the house of anger. She told her father that unless he would marry her to the Jackal-mad she would never leave the room or eat another crumb of food. At length the king agreed to her request, despite the disgrace it would bring him. His ministers, however, advised him to hold a swayamvara, a public assembly of princes at which his daughter could choose her own husband. Then if she still chose the Jackal-mad, he could not be held responsible. So a great swayamvara was held, and when they saw the lovely princess decked in her finest clothes and jewels enter the hall mounted on a white elephant, each hoped that he would receive the garland of roses. But the princess went straight to her corner where the evil-smelling, fly-ridden Jackal-mad stood and put the garland round his neck. Despite the princes' anger, the king was obliged to accept his daughter's public choice.

The princess and the Jackal-mad were therefore married and went to live in a hut which the king had built in the corner of his garden. Their life passed peacefully, except that the nobleman's daughter continually mocked her friend's husband. One day, when the Jackal-mad was bathing, a maid happened to peep at him when he had removed the jackal skin and saw the brilliant jewels about his neck. She quickly called her mistress, who saw how light seemed to radiate from her husband. Seizing the jackal skin, she burnt it and then brought her husband princely clothes. Her joy at discovering his beauty knew no bounds, but he still wished to remain in seclusion. Nevertheless the rumour of his transformation began to spread; one day the nobleman's daughter came to their hut and, disbelieving her friend's good fortune, once more began her taunts. This time, however, was the last. The prince emerged from the hut and cut off her nose and ears, a sign of humiliation. The king, enraged, sent for his daughter; but she replied: 'What right have you to question the actions of my husband? He is the son of Vikramaditya, king of kings.' And now she explained all. Her father, acknowledging himself a petty king beside the son of Vikramaditya, placed his son-in-law on his throne and sat at his feet.

After some time the prince and his wife returned in triumph to Ujjain. He retrieved his father's treasure from the lake and, sending for the honest ministers of the king of Bhuj, made them noblemen in his court. He had his first wife and her lover traced and put to death most horribly. Thereafter he reigned splendidly at Ujjain, a worthy son of Vikramaditya.

Sit and Lakhan

In India legend animals play a significant part, whether in an anthropomorphic role, where they can converse with the human protagonists and share the course of the tale; or as the realistic foes or friends which they represent in everyday life; or again in the symbolic role they hold in religion, embodying good or evil, purity or impurity. In this Santal tale, which seems to amount to a justification for usurpation, animals in all these categories appear. Thus the dogs represent impurity. Snakes, in other legends occupying an ambivalent position as earth godlings, are here realistically the enemies of birds. The birds and the elephant take an active role in furthering the plot and securing the fortune of the heroes. Fortune granted by them is a proof of virtue.

There was once a raja who had two royal wives and a concubine. The elder wife's first son was called Sit and the second was called Lakhan; but in giving birth to Lakhan she died, leaving the care of her two children to her co-wife and the concubine. The king loved his two sons dearly, in memory of their mother, and especially as his second wife had given him no children. But for this very reason the second wife hated her stepchildren and would give them no comfort. The concubine, however, acted as a loving mother towards the children and over the years did her best to protect them from the queen's ill-treatment. She refused to obey when the queen ordered her to prevent the king from seeing hie children. The queen never dared to attack the children openly, but at every opportunity she sought to blacken their characters in the king's eyes. To her fury, however, nothing that her venomous tongue could invent seemed able to shake the king's natural paternal affection. Thus several years passed, during which the queen never lost her hatred for Sit and Lakhan.

One day the queen, feigning illness, took to her bed. The king sent for the best doctors and exorcists in the land, and one after the other they came to examine the queen. She, fearing discovery, would not allow the doctors to touch her, but got the concubine to tie a piece of string to her wrist and let them hold that. Many medicines and remedies were prescribed, but at the end of several days, the queen sent for her husband and began to rail at him for callously neglecting her. These doctors' remedies were of no use whatever; there was only one medicine which could cure her, and she would die unless she had it. When the king had sworn by Kali that he would obtain it for his wife, she told him that she would be cured only by eating the livers of Sit and Lakhan. At first the king could hardly credit that she really meant what she said; but he was bound by his oath, and in the end agreed.

Their conversation was overheard by the concubine and one of the king's sipahis, or armed guards and messengers. The concubine, thinking it kindliest to warn the children, went to Sit and Lakhan and as best might, explained their fate to them. Sit began to weep and protest, but young Lakhan, piously educated under the tutelage of the concubine, accepted with resignation. He said that their father who had given them life had the right to take – it away, and he prepared calmly for the end. Next morning their father had their finest clothes brought for them, but they refused to wear them. Then he sent for three sipahis, among them the one who already knew his intentions, and told them to take the boys out of his sight for ever; then quietly, so the children could not hear, he ordered the sipahis to bring him their livers.

Sit and Lakhan therefore set out with the three sipahis towards the jungle. As they left the palace they passed through the bazaar, where the sipahis,

feeling sorry for the children, bought them sweetmeats. But the children kept the sweet in their hands, for they had no appetite, and the smell attracted two dogs, who followed them for into the jungle. When they had walked a long way, Sit turned to the sipahis and asked them to delay no longer, but to accomplish their purpose. The sipahis, however, told him that they had no intention of obeying the king's orders; but they begged Sit and Lakhan to go far away and never reappear in their father's kingdom. When Sit and Lakhan had walked off alone further into the jungle, the sipahis caught and killed the dogs and took out their livers. On their return they presented these to the sick bed.

Meanwhile Sit and Lakhan spent first night in the jungle at the foot of a tree in which they saw a large bird's nest with two fledglings in it. Bereft as they were themselves, they felt anxious for the fledglings, for as dusk fell no sign was to be seen of the parent bird. Then they heard a rustling in the leaves and, quickly beating with stick, they killed a snake which had been about to devour the fledglings. When at the leaves and, quickly beating with sticks, they killed a snake which had been about to the devour the fledglings told them how the children had saved their lives. At this the parents' happiness knew no bounds, for every year they had raised a brood, only to have all the fledglings devoured by this snake. In their gratitude the parent birds threw down two pieces of food for the by now starving boys. Each piece was magically of food for the by now starving boys. Each piece was magically endowed: whoevei ate the first piece would marry the daughter of a raja, while whoever ate the second piece would spit gold. Si. ate the first piece, and Lakhan the second. Next morning they went on their way and soon became thirsty. While Lakhan went looking for water, Sit sat by the side of the path. Now it

happened that the raja of a nearby kingdom was looking for a husband for his beautiful daughter and heiress, who had just reached marriageable age. According to the custom of the kingdom, a garland was placed on the trunk of an elephant, which was set loose to wander where it chose; wherever it went a large band of attendants followed and watched, for the princess was to marry the man to whom the elephant gave the garland. Sit had not long been resting when this elephant came along the path and without hesitation presented him with the garland. The rejoicing attendants swept up the bewildered boy and took him back to the city, where he was forthwith married to the princess.

Despite his good fortune, Sit was unhappy, for he worried about the fate of his younger brother Lakhan. So his new father-in-law set up a search for Lakhan. Lakhan meanwhile had found refuge with a potter; but the potter, as soon as he found that every time Lakhan opened his mouth he spat gold, had kept the boy virtually prisoner. At last, however, when Sit had paid the potter for looking after his brother, he was forced to give him up. Lakhan came to live in the palace with his brother and was married to the raja's second daughter. With the never-ending gold which poured from his mouth, the kingdom became wealthy and powerful. Meanwhile Sit and Lakhan's father had fallen on evil times: his kingdom had been invaded and he had lost both his fortune and his throne. With his wicked wife he was forced to roam the countryside begging. When they heard this Sit and Lakhan rejoiced, for they could find no forgiveness for their father and stepmother; but they sent for the kind concubine and gave her a good home.

The Boy with the Moon on his Forehead

The need of a king for a son is a recurrent theme in Indian legend. Every Hindu earnestly hopes for a son, for without one his own soul after death cannot receive the proper rites; but for a king with dynastic preoccupations the desire for a son is doubly urgent. Hence the lengths to which kings in legend will go to secure a son; and hence the way in which the son has to prove his legitimacy and worthiness by superhuman attributes and feats of valour. The king with seven wives is one of the most familiar figures of Bengal legend, and the story always pivots on the succession. The present version is typical. Equally typically, each will allow her to produce a son; six of the wives combine against the seventh, so that her son is deformed. In the third main variant, six virtuous wives are ousted by a seventh, who is really a rakshasi. The six wives are blinded and thrown into a pit where one by one each bears a son; but they are forced by hunger ti divide each baby into six and eat it. Only the youngest refuses to eat and so saves her own son; but they are forced by hunger to divide each baby into six and eat it. Only the youngest refuses to eat and so saves her own son; this boy grows up a hero who exposes the wicked queen by conquering her rakshasa relatives and redeems his 'six

mothers'.
The rakshasas which the hero overcomes sometimes represent the hostile and indigenous people of India, but also in some cases the spirits of the ancestors who, by force if necessary, must be made to bend to the heir. By claiming a family relationship to the rakshasas who bar his way the hero is able to overcome their hostility. The sleeping beauty snatched from the rakshasas is thought to represent the raped bride whose marriage alliance may establish the claims of a new ruling house. Here the moon-boy may be opposing the claims of a royal house of the so-called Solar race. The

parallels with the European tales of man-eating ogres are plain, most notably with Jack the Giant-killer: his ogre are too smells out human blood, and is overcome through his seeming stupidity. There was a certain king who reigned in Bengal and had six beautiful and well-born queens, none of whom had given him any children. The king was much grieved and very kind of remedy was tried without avail. His ministers therefore advised the king to marry another wife. Enquiries were made all over the land for a suitable seventh wife, and the king himself took to haunting bathing tanks and other places where women congregated in order to search for himself. One day, having hidden himself from view, the king overheard the conversation of four young girls who were bathing together. Three of them he recognized: they the daughters of his minister, of an important merchant, and of his palace priest. The fourth girl, who greatly surpassed them in beauty, was unknown to him.

The girls fell to talking about their future husbands, and each claimed that her husband would be supremely fortunate. The minister's daughter explained that her clothes never got dirty or worn; The merchant's daughter that the fuel she used for cooking was never consumed or turned to ashes; and the priest's daughter that the rice in her pot replenished itself continuously, no matter how much was eaten. But the fourth girl said that her husband would have cause to rejoice because she would bear twin children, a girl as fair as a goddess and a boy with the moon on his forehead and stars on the palms of his hands.

The king thereupon decided that girl would be his bride and, returning to his palace, asked his minister who she might be. The minister replied that he hardly liked to admit it, but he had given in to his daughter's whim in becoming friendly with the girl on account of her great beauty; for the girl was of the lowest caste and her widowed mother earned her living by collecting cow dung and selling it as fuel in the bazaar. But the king was not to be deterred; his mind was made up and his heart set on the twin children. He therefore announced his intentions to his outraged wives, and sent for the widow so that the marriage could be arranged. Without further delay an auspicious day was set for the wedding, and soon the humble girl become the seventh and favourite queen. The six older

queens, who considered the daughter of a dung-collector too low even to be their servant, could hardly hide their fury when before long the new queen became pregnant. The king suspected their ill-will, so when according to his custom he went to spend six months at his second capital, he gave his young wife a golden bell, telling her to ring it when she felt the pains of childbirth. Wherever he was he would hear it and would immediately be by her side; but he warned her that she must call him for no other reason.

Now the six co-wives had overheard this conversation, so the very day after the king had left they came into the room of the youngest queen and began to admire the golden bell and to ask its purpose. With her trusting nature, the young queen answered that the king had given it to her, telling her that if she rang it he would hear it no matter where he was in his dominions and within minutes be by her side. At this the older queens began to laugh, saying that this must be a joke: how could the king possibly hear the bell-and even if he did, how could he travel so rapidly? Should she not try out her bell? The young queen remembered the king's warning not to ring the bell until she was about to give birth; but the arguments and ridicule of her co-wives overcame her misgivings and she rang the bell. She explained that she had merely wished to try out the bell, but did not add that she had been persuaded to doubt it by the other queens. The king, however, forgave her and departed once more, with a final warning not to misuse the bell again.

Several weeks later the other queens again approached her, saying that the last time the king had been quite close and so had heard the bell: now that he was installed in his other capital many hundreds of miles away, she had better try it again. And so the youngest queen was again persuaded to ring the bell. As before, the king heard the magic bell and hurried to her side; and as before the queen explained but said nothing of how her co-wives had sown the seeds of doubt. This time, however, the king was beside himself with rage and before returning to the distant capital swore that no matter how hard she rang the bell in future, he would not heed it.

Months passed, and at last the queen began to feel the pangs of childbirth. Again and again she rang the bell; but still the king did not come, though he heard it ringing. The delighted co-wives now came to the

young queen and, telling her that it was the custom of the palace that no child should be born in the king's apartments, they had her moved to a hut near the stables. Hare she gave birth to a son with the moon on his forehead and stars on his palms and then to a most beautiful daughter. Now the six queens had bribed the midwife, who had brought with her two newborn pups. Hiding the children, the midwife presented the pups to the queen, telling her that she had given birth to these. Meanwhile the king, repenting of his harshness, had returned to the palace; when he was shown the pups, however his fury redoubled and he had the young queen, weak as she was, thrown out of his palace.

The midwife, deciding the safest way to get rid of the children would be to burn them to ashes, hid them under a large pot waiting to be fired in a potter's kiln at a nearby village. That night as usual the potter set fire to his pots; but miraculously the children escaped harm, and next morning were discovered by the astonished potter and his wife. The potter's wife gave out that she herself had given birth to the twins and proudly displayed them, for such beautiful children had never been seen.

Thus the twins grew up with their loving foster parents, never suspecting their true origin. Their beauty was remarked upon, but no one knew of the moon on the boy's forehead, for he always kept it covered by a turban. At the end of twelve years the potter died and his faithful wife, thinking the children old enough to fend for themselves, threw herself on his funeral pyre. The two children sold the potter's goods and went to the bazaar in the

city. As they entered the whole bazaar seemed to light up. Observing this happy portent, the bazaar merchants begged them to stay and built them a little house in the bazaar, where they looked after them kindly. With the money inherited from the potter, they helped the boy to buy a horse — not an ordinary horse but a fine steed of the *pakshiraj* tribe, who were known as kings of the birds because they could gallop as fast as the wind. On this horse the boy used to go hunting in the neighbouring forests. One day, while pursuing a deer, he chanced to come across the king and his party, who were hunting in the same forest. Just as he came into view of the king, he shot an arrow at the deer, loosing it with such force that his turban fell off. At once the forest was bathed in an unearthly brilliance. The king observed this and immediately thought of the son he had hoped for, who was to have the moon on his forehead. But before he could speak, the boy had galloped off into the forest and was lost from sight. The king, returning to his palace, was full of gloomy thoughts and admitted the cause to his six solicitous wives. They immediately took fright and sent for the midwife to question her. She of course swore that she had seen the children burnt with her own eyes; but privately she began to worry and to make enquiries. Soon she discovered that a brother and sister of wondrous beauty were living in the bazaar and she realized that destiny had intervened to thwart her and the queens who had bribed her.

The midwife therefore entered the house in the bazaar while the boy was away hunting, and convinced the girl that she was an aunt who had left the city shortly before the birth of her and her twin brother and had just returned. With many endearments, she flattered the girl and made much of her beauty; and told her that to set off her loveliness the only flower good enough was the *kataki.* She should get her brother to obtain some for her and plant them by their house. The girl had never seen or heard of such a flower and, her vanity aroused, enquired eagerly where it might be obtained. So the midwife, sure that the noble boy would risk his life to obtain *kataki* flowers if his sister were to ask for them, explained that they grew only in one place, a land on the other side of the ocean which was guarded by seven hundred rakshasas. When she had gone, the boy with the moon on his forehead returned from hunting. Though he doubted whether they had an aunt, his beloved sister's eagerness to adorn herself with *kataki* flowers persuaded him, and next morning he set out in search of them.

His swift horse quickly brought him to the edge of a dense forest far from any human habitation and stretching into the distance as far as the eye could see. Soon he saw the first hideous rakshasas

looming in the distance. Now the boy was endowed not only with beauty and courage, but also with intelligence. So at once, before the rakshasas could see him, he shot some deer and rhinoceros. Then he went near the rakshasas and called out: 'Here I am, Aunt, here!' A vast rakshasi came towards him, and said: 'You are the boy with the moon on his forehead and stars on his palms. We knew you were coming, and were eager to eat you up. But as you have called me aunt, I shall do you no harm.' Then the boy brought forward the deer and rhinoceros carcasses. The rakshasi's eyes lit up as she recceived this gift; in a moment she had devoured them all. Then she turned once more to the boy and asked him how she could help him, and he explained that he had come to get *kataki* flowers for his sister. The rakshasi warned him of the difficulties; but she told him that if he were determined to get them, he should first go to his uncle on the northern side of the forest.

Fearlessly the boy rode on through the forest, and as he approached the northern edge shot more deer and rhinoceros. Then he called out: 'Here I am, Uncle. My aunt has sent me to you.' The rakshasa was disarmed by the claim of kinship just as his sister had been. When he had eaten his fill of deer and rhinoceros, he told the boy that the way to the *kataki* gardens was beset with obstacles. First he would come to an impenetrable forest of thorny *kachiri* lilies, so dense that not even a mouse could pass through it. Standing before it, he should say, 'Mother *kachiri*, make way for me, or I shall die', and a passage would open up before him. Then he would come to an ocean, and should say, 'Mother ocean, make way for me, or I shall die', and the waters would part, leaving a dry channel for him to ride along. And on the other side of ocean, he would find the *kataki* gardens; once there, his real difficulties would begin, for the flowers themselves were guarded by seven hundred rakshasas, and no one could advise him how to escape their fierce and watchful eyes.

The boy with the moon on his forehead was not to

be frightened by the final warning and boldly rode on. Following the rakshasa's advice, he called in turn on 'Mother *kachiri*' and 'Mother ocean', who immediately parted before him, so that soon found himself in the *kataki* gardens. There before him stood a palace, which he entered. Wandering from room to room, he thought at first that the palace was altogether deserted. But at last he came to a room where, on a golden bed, slept a girl whose beauty surpassed even that of his sister. Softly he spoke to her, then loudly; but she did not stir. Then he noticed two sticks lying on her bed: a silver one at her feet and a golden one at her head. He picked them up to look more closely and then replaced them; but in doing so he reversed their positions and the beauty woke.

No sooner had she opened her eyes than she told him she knew who he was, and warned him not to remain a moment longer in the palace, which was the home of the seven hundred rakshasas: as soon as they returned from hunting they would kill and eat him. Then she told him how she came to be the only human being ever to remain alive in the rakshasa kingdom. She was a royal princess called Pushpavati who had been snatched away from her earthly home together with great numbers of her father's subjects, all of whom had been devoured. By the time her turn had come, however, a certain rakshasi had become fond of her and had saved her.

Now she lived under the protection of this rakshasi, who every day when she went out to hunt with the others would put her to sleep with the sticks and every night would wake her to sleep with the sticks and every night would wake her by reversing them. Hearing her story, the boy became determined not only to get the *kataki* flowers, but also to save her. That night before the rakshasa returned, he put Pushpavati to sleep again and hid under a heap of *kataki* flowers. Her guardian entered, woke Pushpavati, and declared that she smelt strange human flesh. The princess assured her that she was the only human being in the palace and began to flatter and cosset her. However, soon she fell to weeping. When the rakshasi asked her why she wept, she explained that she was thinking how sad she would be when her dear guardian died. Touched by this demonstration, the foolish rakshasi dried her tears and said: 'Do you not know that we rakshasas are as good as immortal? It is ordained that only a person with a moon on his forehead and stars on the palms of his hands can harm us — and how can such a human being exist? Then in order to kill us, he would have to dive to the bottom of the tank in the middle of the *kataki* gardens and bring up the wooden box which lies there. This would have to be opened without letting the male and female bee which live in it escape. Then he would have to kill them without letting one drop of blood fall to the ground. If he should let a single drop fall to the ground, he himself would be instantly torn into seven hundred pieces. Now how could any human being fulfil these conditions, even if he knew of them? And only if they were fulfilled would a single rakshasa die.' With that, the rakshasi contentedly went sleep.

Next morning, when the rakshasas had left the palace and the boy had woken Pushpavati, she told him every detail of this conversation. Immediately he went to the tank, dived in, brought out the box, caught the bees, and crushed them between his

palms, rubbing the blood all over his body so not a drop could fall. Now when the boy touched the box in which their life was preserved, each of the seven hundred rakshasas began to run towards the tank. But the boy had foreseen this danger and carried out the instructions so quickly that they had no time to reach him. As soon as the bees were dead, with the sound of a whirlwind, all the rakshasas breathed their last and fell like crumbling mountains to the earth. Then the boy with the moon on his forehead gathered up a great bunch of *kataki* flowers, lifted the princess on to his horse, and they quickly rode back home, where the boy presented his delighted sister with her flowers and with his bride.

Next day the boy went hunting according to his wont. Once more he encountered the king's hunting party, and as before he lost his turban while shooting, thus uncovering the moon on his forehead and dazzling all about him. This time, however, the king acted swiftly in telling the boy to stop. The boy asked him to come to his house in the bazaar if he wished to speak; and the king, impelled by his premonition, agreed to this strange request from a subject.

On the following day he came to the little house in the bazaar, where he was greeted by Pushpavati, who knew the whole story and recounted it to the king. At once overjoyed and incensed, the king without delay allotted their just deserts to his six barren and wicked wives, who were buried alive in a great pit; then he sent to the bazaar or his seventh queen, and reinstated her. As for the boy with the moon on his forehead, he shared the rule of the kingdom with his father and lived happily with his beautiful wife and sister.

Tales from Western India

Vikramaditya

Raja Vikram is a favourite figure of Indian legend. Admired for his great powers and respected for his just rule, he is commonly known as Vikramaditya, or Vikram of the eternal, celestial light. He is always associated with his vizir, Butti, a man whose faithfulness and character, which was complementary to his own, ensured a great reign. From their friendship comes the common expression in India, 'they love each other like the raja and the vizir'. In legend, Vikramaditya, like Solomon and Harun al-Rashid of the Arabian

Nights, is known for his outstanding wisdom; he is equally famous, however, because he was incurably fond of wandering. His wisdom was the gift of Ganesa, god of wisdom, who also gave him the power to enter other bodies. Vikram is said to have received the power to fly from Kubera, god of wealth and of hidden treasure.

Vikramaditya reigned at Ujjain, a city near the Narmada river, in the Vindhya mountain region, and he is identified with the founder of the Samvat era, who ruled there in the first century B.C. and extended his power as far west as Kabul. Alternatively, he is identified with Chandragupta II of the Gupta dynasty, who reigned at Magadha from A.D. 375 to 413; or again with Harsha, who defeated the Mlekkas in A.D. 544 and was a worshipper of the sun. This identification would provide a clue to his relationship with his vizir Butti, whose name means Light.

In all versions of the Vikramaditya legend the hero wanders so far that he seems lost for a time to those left at home; yet everywhere he goes he is recognized as a mighty king. This reflects popular wonder at the vast extent of Vikram's dominions.

A common storyteller's device is the overhearing of speaking animals; its introduction in the legend of Vikram has a special point in that understanding the language of animals is a sign of wisdom - as in the case of King Solomon. The fact that Buccoli shares the gift with Vikramaditya, together with the prophetic dream through which she identifies her future husband, proves her worthiness as queen. In Indian legends brides often choose their husbands by means of supernatural signs, are cast out by their parents, then justify themselves and their choice and reinstate their royal husbands. Such stories no doubt originate in justification of dynastic marriages; the bond cemented here between Anar Rani, the first wife, and Buccoli, the second, confirms this.

The pomegranate is a native of North Africa and Western Asia, not India, so that Anar Rani's origin in the 'Pomegranate country' indicates that she too came from a distant land; far from India and hard of access. The difficulties put in the way of her suitors bears this out.

Vikramaditya was the son of a pious raja who devoted much of his wealth to building a magnificent marble temple in whose shrine stood a pure gold image of the god Ganesa. Shortly after the completion of the temple, while Vikram was still a young boy, both his parents died, leaving the conduct of the kingdom in the hands of a trusted minister during Vikram's minority. Vikram was brought up with the minister's son Butti, and they became inseparable friends. Both were intelligent and imaginative, and Vikram's fanciful tendencies

were nicely balanced by his friend's good sense. When Vikram assumed power the kingdom flourished under his and Butti's joint direction and Vikram became famed for his generosity to the needy. The temple built by Vikram's parents, however, stood forgotten at some distance from the capital and became overgrown by jungle plants. One day Butti suggested to Vikram that as an act of piety he should restore the temple. Vikram immediately agreed and the full glory of the forgotten temple was uncovered. He and Butti began to sleep in the temple every night. One night his father appeared to Vikram in a dream and told him of a vast hoard of treasure buried at the foot of the votive tower of lights in front of the temple. But his father went on to warn him that he would incur Ganesa's wrath in removing the treasure unless he first performed a supreme act of devotion to the god. With a rope and a basket, he should climb to the top of the tower of lights, whose base was surrounded by seven rows of sharp blades; he should attach one

end of the rope to the top of the tower and the other to the basket, twist the rope three times, put his head into the basket and allow himself to fall, at the same time cutting the rope. Then he should put his faith in Ganesa to save him from falling on to the blades. Next morning Vikram told Butti of this strange dream, and his normally cautious friend advised him to follow his father's instructions. Vikram did so and sure enough, as he was falling towards the deadly blades, Ganesa had mercy on him. Disguising himself as an old woman, he ran out of the temple and caught Vikram in his arms; then, after bearing him safely down to earth, he once more disappeared. Vikram now went on to have the base of the tower excavated, and a great treasure of gold, diamonds, rubies, sapphires, emeralds, turquoise and pearls was found. He took none of this for himself, however, but sold it and gave the proceeds to the poor.

Some time later Vikram was again sleeping in the temple when his father appeared in a second dream, telling his that knowledge was of no value without wisdom and that he should come to the temple daily to receive Ganesa's instruction in wisdom. Vikram once more followed his father's advise and every day took instruction from the god of wisdom, until the day arrived when Ganesa declared that he had learnt as much wisdom as was fitting for a mortal. As a parting gift Ganesa offered to grant whatever

Vikram named: wealth, long life, happiness, or whatever he chose. After a day's reflection, Vikram returned to Ganesa. He had none of the usual human ambitions, for he accepted his destiny as a man; but he requested a power he had long dreamt of; the ability to enter with his soul and mind the body of another being - bird, man or beast, together with the means to prevent his own body from decaying in the meantime. So Ganesa taught the great raja how to accomplish his wish, trusting that with the wisdom he had acquired he would not misuse his powers.

Now it so happened that a wily carpenter's son had all this time been hiding outside the temple and listening as best he could to Vikram's course of instruction. Naturally, he was overjoyed at sharing Ganesa's final gift; but because he had learnt the lessons imperfectly he took no heed of the instructions for preserving the natural body.

At this time, and for some years past, all the local princes were striving to gain the and of a beautiful little princess, Anar Rani, the 'Pomegranate Princess', so called because she lived with her two maidservants in the three great fruits of a pomegranate tree. Every day the tree would bend and the fruits would open to release the three girls into the gardens, and every evening they would once more retire within the fruits. Anar Rani's parents had decreed that she should marry only the prince who could pluck the three pomegranates and bear them away. But the garden in which the tree stood was surrounded by seven hedges of sharp blades, so that all the princes who had sought to win this fairest of all princesses had perished miserably. The prize of Anar Rani was an obvious challenge to Vikram with his new powers: he quickly entered the body of a dead parrot, flew to the pomegranate country and over the seven hedges of sharp blades, plucked the three pomegranate and bore them back in his beak to Ujjain. There he resumed his human form and married Anar Rani.

Despite his happy marriage, however, Vikram soon felt restless, and decided once more to take the form of a parrot and to see the world. Warning his wife and Butti that he would appear as if dead and might be gone for as long as a year, he entered the body of a handsome parrot and flew away. As soon as the carpenter's son heard of the king's 'illness', he realized what had happened and decided himself to enter Vikram's body. Thus Vikram appeared to revive immediately, and this aroused the suspicions of Butti. He advised Anar Rani to test the 'king' by giving him coarse food; the carpenter's son, used to such fare, made no complaint and so gave himself away. Anar Rani would have nothing more to do with him. Being a king was thus not so pleasant after all; but alas the carpenter's son could not return to his former self, for his old body had by now decayed.

Meanwhile the real Vikram had become the leader of a thousand parrots living in a tree in the jungle. One day, through ignoring Vikram's wise counsel, they were nearly caught by a hunter; but Vikram devised a ruse whereby they all escaped. Vikram himself, though, they allowed to fall into the hunter's hands. Vikram saved his life by telling the astonished hunter that he could be sold for a thousand gold mohurs in the nearby town. A merchant paid the sum, intrigued by the bird, who claimed he would earn it.

Vikram soon kept his promise for, by dispensing wise remarks and advice, he brought customers from far and wide, who made the merchant's fortune in the space of a week. After some time a strange case came before the local judge and then the raja: Champa Rani, a well-known and rich dancing girl, having overheard a poor woodcutter tell his friends of a dream about giving Champa Rani a wedding gift of a thousand gold mohurs, claimed that they were in fact married and that he owed her the sum. The raja himself was at a loss, and it was decided to refer the case to the judgement of the wise parrot. Vikram easily demonstrated that just as Champa was unable to extract a thousand mohurs from a sealed bottle without breaking it, so a woodcutter with beggarly earnings could not possibly owe such a sum. Champa Rani had to admit defeat, but threatened sooner or later to bite off the parrot's head. Vikram for his part warned her that he would make her a beggar: she would raze her own house and for shame kill herself.

Some weeks later the merchant's son was married and Champa Rani danced at the feast. The merchant offered her any reward she named. Quickly she asked for the parrot, and the merchant was forced to give her the source of his fortune. As soon as she arrived home she ordered her maids to cook the parrot and to bring her first the head to eat. Vikram pretended to be dead and they plucked his feathers. Then, when their backs were turned, he made his escape into a waste pipe. The maids therefore presented Champa Rani with a chicken's head, which she ate with great delight.

Vikram, meanwhile, was forced to remain in the waste pipe and live off the scraps washed away, for he could not fly until his wing feathers grew again. At last, however, he was able to escape to a temple in the jungle, where he hid behind the idol. This very temple was Champa Rani's favourite place of prayer, where she called upon her god to transport her body and soul to heaven, without the indignity of death. And so, on her next visit, Vikram was able to impersonate the god and instruct the dancing girl that her wish would be granted if she would sell her possessions and give the money to the poor, pay off her servants and burn her house to the ground. Then she should come back a week later, when she would rise to heaven. Champa made speed to do as she was bidden, and invited the whole town to witness her transfiguration the following week. Thus it was in front of a great crowd that Vikram was able to emerge and taunt Champa Rani. She now saw that the parrot's words had come true and that she was destitute; in despair she beat her head on the ground till she died.

It was now two years since Vikram had departed from his own country and for the past six months Butti had been searching the world for him. It happened that Butti was among the crowd who had come to watch Champa Rani's ascension to heaven. He and Vikram recognized each other and returned together to Ujjain. It was not, however, possible for

Vikram to regain his human form immediately, for it was first necessary to dispose of the carpenter's son. After some time the false raja proposed to the vizir that they stage a match between their fighting rams. It became apparent that Butti's ram was winning, and the 'raja', remembering his supernatural powers, decided to enter the body of his own ram to give it strength. As soon as the real Vikram saw what had happened, he entered his own body. Meanwhile Butti beheaded the ram, thereby killing the carpenter's son.

Great was the rejoicing of Butti and of Anar Rani at the return of Vikramaditya, who now promised his queen that he would never again take the form of a parrot and fly away. But Vikram was unable to restrain his restlessness for long, and took to wandering about the nearby jungle alone. One hot day, while on such a walk, he sat down under a tree to rest, and while he slept a cobra saw his open mouth and, thinking it a cool cranny, crawled in. When Vikram awoke he called to the cobra to get out of his throat, but it would not move. With all his wisdom, with all his powers, Vikram was the most miserable creature alive. At last, in despair, he ran away into the jungle.

Butti reflected sadly that Vikram's the gift of the god, was negated by the unnatural power which he had wished upon himself, so that he himself was unhappy and his kingdom lacked firm government.

The vizir sent out searchers to bring the raja black, but Vikram was nowhere to be found. Finally Butti himself left the kingdom in search of his friend.

During this time Vikram had wandered as far as a distant kingdom and sat with the beggars at the gate of the raja's palace. Now the raja's daughter, Buccoli, had for some time been refusing her many suitors because she had dreamt of the man she was destined to marry, and she informed her parents that his name was Raja Vikram. They had never heard of any prince called Vikram, but agreed to wait, thinking he might be greater than any prince they had heard of. Imagine their horror, then, when as soon as Vikram sat among the beggar sat their gate, Buccoli pointed out this bundle of rags as her destined husband. The 'beggar' revealed that his name was indeed Raja

Vikram, but the parents were still horror-struck. Though they finally allowed the marriage to take place, they banished their daughter and her husband from their palace.

Buccoli and Vikram therefore lived in the jungle, where Vikram continued to suffer from the cobra in his throat, while Buccoli suffered from the unaccustomed rough life and from seeing her husband's pain. One night, while she lay awake trying to think of a remedy, she overheard two cobras speaking to each other. One cobra told the other the story of Vikram and his wife and explained how they had come to this pass. He then remarked how easily Vikram's wife could rid him of the snake of she would only hang Vikram upside down over a boiling cauldron of coconut oil and marking nuts-just as she could with the same brew fumigate one of them in his hole and, having killed him, take the treasure he guarded. Next morning Buccoli lost no time in doing as the cobra had said, and thus restored Vikram to health and gained a vast treasure of gold, silver and jewels. With her now handsome husband she returned to her parents' palace, where they were welcomed.

There they also found a visitor: a vizir from a distant land who had been searching for his missing raja for twelve years. It was Butti. All returned together to Vikramaditya's kingdom, where Anar Rani welcomed the husband she had begun to mourn and her new co-wife, who had restored him to health and to his kingdom. Vikram, for his part, promised never again to leave his kingdom. He reigned wisely and well and was beloved his subjects. His friendship with his vizir Butti never faded, and they both lived to a ripe age.

Guru Gugga, The Rajput of Bagar

Guru Gugga is one of the most ambiguous figures in Indian legend. He is a Rajput hero of Bikaner (called Bagar in the stories, meaning the 'prairies' of northern Rajputana), an outpost of civilization on the southern edge of the Thar desert. His legend ascribes to him miracles and great military exploits, notably against Firoz Shah of Delhi when the latter supported the claims of his half-brothers. It also gives him the attributes of a snake deity who can cure snakebite and is the consort of Mother Earth, so forming a link between the benign and the malignant spirits of the earth; and of a Hindu convert to Islam (the conversion enabling him to be assimilated to Mother Earth). He is now popularly one of the principal Moslem saints, known as Zahir Pir, meaning 'saint apparent'; or Zahria Pir ('poisonous saint'), because as a baby he sucked a snake's head. Though the legend connects Gugga through his mother with the Rajputs ruling in Kabul and in Ghazni before the conquest by the Moslems in A.D. 662, in life he was probably a Hindu leader of the Chauhan Rajputs, who died fighting against Mahmud of Ghazni in about A.D. 1000. Guru Gorakhnath, a common *deus ex machina* of folk tales, was in real life the Brahminical opponent of the religious reformers about in A.D. 1400. His role in the legend of Guru Gugga is entwined with various stock motifs employed by the bards to advance their stories, notably magic pregnancy, the wicked stepmother and prophetic dreams.

Jewar, raja of Bagar, was an able and virtuous ruler who was married to two sisters, Bachhal and Kachhal, daughters of the leader of the Chauhan Rajputs at Ghazni. But there was no happiness for Jewar, for his wives or for his kingdom, for neither Bachhal, his favourite, nor Kachhal had presented him with an heir. Both queens had implored the gods for the boon of a son, particularly Bachhal, who for twelve years had been praying to the Guru Gorakhnath to act as intermediary for her Plea. As for Jewar, he tried to comfort his wives, putting his faith in the mercy of Vishnu and sustained by the prophecy of the palace priest Rangachar that there would be three sons.

At last, on an auspicious day, word came to the palace that Guru Gorakhnath resplendent in his saintly beauty, had entered the royal garden. Jewar hurried out to greet him and to present him with palanquins laden with costly gifts. That evening, Bachhal went to pay her respects to the saint, presenting him with a dish of pearls and begging him for his help. Guru Gorakhnath, moved by her plight and by her pious resignation to the divine will, bade her pray to Brahma and Vishnu and return later. Meanwhile Kachhal, hearing of Bachhal's visit, rose early next morning, dressed herself up as Bachhal and visited the saint, obtaining from him two seeds, through eating which she would conceive two sons. Bachhal again visited Gorakhnath and at first was spurned by him for desiring yet another son; but soon the deceit was revealed and the Guru presented Bachhal with a third magical seed. Kachhal, he explained to her, would be cursed for her deceit: her sons would live only twelve years and they would be the cause of her own death. Bachhal's son Gugga, on the other hand, would be beautiful, brave and a miracle worker; kings and peoples would bow before him.

Bachhal's happiness was short-lived, however, for Jewar's sister Sabir Dei, prompted by Kachhal, became suspicious of Bachhal's prolonged and frequent visits to Gorakhnath even at midnight, and accused her of infidelity. She so poisoned her brother's mind that he would have killed Bachhal instantly; but Guru Gorakhnath miraculously intervened to prevent the dagger leaving its scabbard and her life was saved. And so, accompanied only by a driver, Bachhal set out on a bullock cart to return to her parents at Ghazni.

As they made their long journey across the desert under the hot sun, they came to a stream where Bachhal rested while the driver watered the bullocks. Suddenly a snake emerged from the

waters and bit the bullocks. In an instant the poison convulsed the mighty bullocks, who fell dead before their horrified eyes. The frail queen could hardly endure the journey across the mountains to Ghazni by bullock cart; how could she possibly continue on foot? Yet the driver could not abandon her. He too seemed caught up in her evil fate-and if Bachhal was innocent, how much more so was he. Yet both seemed fated to die of exposure, if they were not first to share the swift and tortured end of the bullocks. Bachhal at once perceived her plight and, bewailing her lot, fainted away in anguish.

As she lay by the river bank Gugga spoke to her from the womb. He told her to cut a branch of the nearby Nim tree, whose bitter leaves are considered a specific against snakebite, and to call on Gorakhnath and make him an offering. Rising up, Bachhal followed the guidance of her miraculous dream, whereupon the bullocks revived and carried her on to her parental home. At Ghazni, Bachhal explained to her mother the depths of her unhappiness at her husband's unjust suspicions and his rejection of her in the twelfth month of her pregnancy (its length was a miraculous sign). Now Gugga's voice was again heard from the womb calling on Gorakhnath to succour Bachhal and to show Jewar a miracle and so persuade him to recall his wife, for it would be shameful for Gugga to be born away from home. No sooner had Gugga spoken than his father dreamt that evil would befall him unless he recalled his wife. When he awoke his minister advised that unless he reinstated Bachhal the Chauhan Rajputs would become his enemies and he would lose his life. With due ceremony, therefore, and escorted by a large cavalcade, Jewar and his priest Rangachar set out to fetch Bachhal. Jewar was well received at Ghazni, but he soon announced his wish to return to Bagar. As he left the fort with Bachhal, propitious omens were seen: a partridge calling on the right and a snake appearing on the left. Rangachar foretold that an auspicious time for the birth would be Bhadhon, the month of snakes, and that the infant would be a miracle worker. So as soon as Gugga was born Jewar proclaimed the child his heir and made the kingdom over to him.

Thus Gugga's life ushered in propitiously and nothing disturbed his mother's tranquillity until the child, true to his Rajput warrior ancestry, began to seek adventure; for however young, a Rajput boy cannot remain still for long. Rising early one day, Gugga set out hunting. The excitement of the chase led him further and further away from home, and as the sun rose high Gugga became parched with thirst. At last he reached a well where some women were drawing water and asked one for a drink. But the woman was a Brahmin and thus of higher caste than the warrior Kshatriyas, and she refused

Gugga, on the grounds that his lips would defile her pitcher. As she walked away, one pitcher balanced on top of the other, Gugga took revenge for the insult by praying to Gorakhnath and loosing an arrow, which broke both pitchers and drenched the woman. Weeping at the humiliation, she pronounced a curse on Gugga: 'May you neither prosper nor live: may your children die in infancy.' Too late, Bachhal interceded on behalf of the thoughtless child: the curse had been pronounced, and ignorance could not excuse such an insult to a Brahmin.

Nevertheless, the kingdom of Raja Jewar prospered and he and his son Gugga were renowned far and wide. Raja Sanja of Kamrup in Assam was at this time looking for a suitable husband for his daughter Siriyal and sent off his priest Gunman to try to arrange a match with Gugga. The journey was long and arduous and little to Gunman's taste. After four

months, as he struggled on towards Jewar's kingdom, Gunman uttered the wish that Siriyal should suffer as he had suffered on her behalf. Thus both Siriyal and Gugga were irredeemably cursed. Nevertheless, all seemed well at first. When Gunman reached Jewar's palace his suit on behalf of Siriyal was welcomed and the betrothal arranged. Hardly had Gunman returned to bring the glad news to Sanja, however, than a letter arrived from Bagar announcing the death of Jewar. Sanja concluded that the royal house of Bagar was unlucky and forthwith broke off the betrothal. A double grief of bereavement and of the slight to her son now assailed Bachhal, once again confronted by her unlucky destiny and suspecting her sister Kachhal's part in it.

Gugga, seeing her weeping, went off into the jungle, made a flute, and played it to call Gorakhnath. The flute-playing entranced the birds and beasts of the jungle, all except Vasuki the snake king, because it stirred all the snakes of the world into wakefulness. Vasuki therefore sent his priest Tatig Naga to see who Gugga was and why he was playing. Gugga explained why he had come to the jungle to seek from his guardian Gorakhnath redress against Sanja of Kamrup. Now Gorakhnath had special powers over snakes so, on hearing that Gugga was under his protection, Vasuki ordered Tatig Naga to obey Gugga's commands. Calling on the help of

Gorakhnath, Tatig Naga pledged himself to go to distant Dhupnagar, Sanja's city, whose patron deity was the Great Mother Devi, and there to arrange the renewal of Siriyal's betrothal to Gugga.

Tatig Naga took the form of a Brahmin beggar and before long was lying in the garden of Sanja's palace, pretending to rest. As soon as Siriyal and her seven maids appeared, Tatig asked for alms. But Siriyal scornfully gave him only a dirty and valueless coin and Tatig refused it. Siriyal took no notice but got on her swing and began enjoying herself. Immediately Tatig turned himself back into a snake, climbed into the tree and was about to strike Siriyal when she saw him and fell off the swing. Later, however, when she was bathing, Tatig had his second chance and bit her toe. Siriyal fell into mortal illness and Sanja sent in turn for all the snake charmers of the land, But none was able to cure her. Tatig, having turned back into a Brahmin, discovered this from a water bearer and sent word to the palace that he was a snake charmer. Then, calling on Guru Gorakhnath for aid, he entered the palace, where the princess lay covered with a shroud. Promising the grief stricken Sanja to cure his daughter, Tatig obtained from him a written promise that he would marry Siriyal to Gugga. Then he administered the branch of a Nim tree and sucked the poison out of Siriyal's toe, whereupon the princess came to life. Sanja in his

joy proclaimed that the wedding would take place with a great display of wealth in seven day's time.

After a tearful farewell from her mother, Siriyal and her husband set out on the long journey home. Gorakhnath himself, having pronounced a blessing on Sanja, accompanied the newly married pair and did not leave them until they had reached Bagar. Here her presented Siriyal to his devotee Bachhal, and assured her that now her troubles were at an end.

Some time after their return to Bagar, Guru Gugga expressed his wish to see his half-brother Urjan and Surjan, the sons of Kachhal, whom he had not seen since their birth twelve years before. When they met, Surjan sought to flatter Gugga with sweet words about his grief at not having seen him for so long; but he quickly followed this with a request for a share in the hereditary property. Gugga reproached his half-brothers for his covetousness and for his blind and bitter thoughts. He asked Bachhal to persuade Surjan of his folly; but when she sought reason with Surjan, pointing out that all material things are vain illusion and of no profit, he replied by begging her, if she was so upright and pious in dismissing worldly values, to concede his right to a half share in the property. Why did she not give the same advice to her son Gugga? In his heart, Surjan decided to kill Gugga.

Again Surjan approached his half-brother smilingly and invited him to come hunting, as befitted a Rajput warrior. Gugga agreed, and the three brothers set out. Thirsty after riding hard all day, they found that they were lost, and surrounded on all sides by jungle. Gugga, wondering how they had come to such a pass, called on Gorakhnath and sat down with his head in his hands . Then, while Urjan sat beside him and spoke comforting words, Surjan came up behind and tried to cut off Gugga's head; but each of his two strokes was parried by Fate. Gugga, realizing his danger, called once more on Gorakhnath and with his divine aid quickly cut off the head first Urjan and then of Surjan. Attaching the heads to his saddle, Gugga then found his way out of the jungle. As soon as he arrived at his palace he showed the heads of his would-be murderers to their mother Kachhal, who at the sight died of grief. Bachhal's reaction was hardly less dramatic, for when she heard the news she banished Gugga from her sight for ever, and invoked the curse of Gorakhnath on him if he disobeyed.

Gugga, as an honourable Rajput, was obliged to obey his mother's command, even if she repented of it. He therefore called on Mother Earth to open and swallow him up. She replied that she could not receive him, a Hindu, for while Moslems go into the earth, Hindus must be burnt on a pyre. She told him that if he learnt the Moslem creed she would take him, despite the curses of his wife Siriyal. So Gugga went to Ajmer in the Aravalli Hills and there learnt the Moslem creed from Rattan Haji (the 'Pilgrim')

.Then he again called on Mother Earth to swallow him up so that he might fulfil his vow and thus not lose his honour. As he spoke, his acceptance into the Moslem faith was confirmed, for Earth opened and took him to herself.

The Workings of Destiny

The Indian idea of destiny seems to lie somewhere between that of the Greeks, where man is a pawn, and the notion of tragedy as self-inflicted doom. Man is born into the condition he deserves according to his actions in previous incarnations. None must help him to rebel, for merit is gained through carrying out the duties of his station. In this legend the seeds of dishonour, once sown, grow ineluctably to cause the downfall of Jetpur.

A fakir had been receiving alms of milk from a cobbler of the city of Jetpur who hoped that one day the fakir would grant him a boon. Though the fakir should have known that the merit the cobbler achieved through keeping him alive was sufficient reward, he nevertheless offered a boon, and the cobbler asked for control over a jinn. At once the fakir saw that he had made a mistake: the result was bound to cause suffering to himself, to the cobbler and to others, for cobblers are of very low caste and the lowly cannot command the great person. But the fakir had promised, and the cobbler would not be convinced. So the cobbler acquired control over a jinn for three months. The first of the holy man's fears was soon justified, for as soon as he had obtained his boon, the mean-minded cobbler, incapable of gratitude, abandoned his benefactor, who starved to death.

The humble cobbler had heard of the fabled beauty of the princess of Ahmedabad in distant Gujarat and wished to feast his eyes on her; so each evening when the jinn appeared on his left shoulder to receive his orders he had the princess transported in her royal bed to his small, evil smelling hut. Overawed by her beauty, he never touched or spoke to the princess who, for her part, every night fainted away in fear and woke next morning in her own apartments at the Shah-i-bagh palace thinking she had had an evil dream. Rapidly her beauty began to fade away and at last she confided her dream to her mother, the Sultana.

That night her mother slept with her and saw that the princess and her bed really did disappear. The

Sultan vowed vengeance on the abductor of his daughter and instructed her next night to discover his name and his city. When for the first time the princess spoke to him and asked him about himself, the foolish cobbler told her all: that his name was Gordhan and his city Jetpur; and then, as usual, he had the princess transported home.

As soon as the Sultan learnt this, he set out with his army to raze the city of Jetpur to the ground; but while he was marching towards Jetpur, of course, nothing could stop the nightly abduction of his daughter.

Now Bavawala, the king of Jetpur, was a Kathi, who rivalled the Rajputs in their reputation for martial prowess. He prided himself on being the bravest man in Jetpur and the readiest to commence battle. One evening an approaching dust cloud warned him of the Sultan's attack; but his resolve was only strengthened by the threat.

As he was wondering who could be mounting an attack on him, he heard a woman wailing by the river. He went to her and discovered that it wan no woman but an apsara, one of the divine dancing girls of Indra's heaven; owing to his great virtue, Bavawala was able to see her. She told him that, knowing of the coming battle and of the king's valour, she had vowed herself to the man who struck the first blow, thinking it could be none other than Bavawala. But now the lords of destiny had revealed to her that the first blow would be struck by Desla, a low-caste man whose task was to beat the drums announcing the start of battle. Bavawala assured the apsara that he would strike the first blow and, to make sure, he would have Desla imprisoned with his drum at the top of a tower. But the apsara could not be comforted, for she knew that one's destiny cannot be avoided and that she must suffer for her own foolish vow and the gratuitous boon given by the fakir to the cobbler. She then told the story of the cobbler and explained that Bavawala too would suffer as a result of it.

Bavawala, however, was convinced that men could guide their destinies and that some mistakes could be rectified; so, having learnt the cobbler's name and where he lived, he went straight to his hut and entered, discovering Gordhan as he gazed at the princess. Now Gordhan, with the help of the jinn, was far more powerful than the king, but being a lowly man he was incapable of using power well; Bavawala, however, was born to command and did so unthinkingly. He at once ordered Gordhan to summon his jinn and to have him transfer the princess to the finest apartment of Jetpur palace; and then to tell the jinn that in future he should obey the king's commands alone. Gordhan, terrified, obeyed unquestioningly.

Next, as dawn approached, Bavawala ordered the jinn to transport the Sultan and his ten senior officers to the palace, and this was done, to the fury of the Sultan and the mystification of his army. Soon Bavawala explained to the Sultan all that had happened and assured him that he had safely rescued the princess, and that what had occurred was not his fault but the fakir's. The Sultan was not easily persuaded to abandon his vow of vengeance, but finally agreed to send his ten officers to call off the attack in return for Gordhan's banishment and the gift of three villages to the mosque, so that no fakir in future should be driven by hunger to become indebted to a man beneath his contempt. The Sultan agreed to remain as hostage but begged that his daughter should be returned to her mother by the jinn. Bavawala consented and the bargain was made. He called upon the jinn, but the jinn did not appear. He called upon Gordhan to summon the jinn, but again no jinn appeared. The three months of his service to Gordhan had elapsed that very night. The Sultan was absolved from his part of the agreement; nothings could stop the onrush of his army.

The abduction of the Sultan and his officers spurred his troops to extraordinary feats. One of them scaled the very tower in which Desla was beating his drum. Outraged, Desla fell upon him and both were killed. Thus Desla struck the first blow of battle and his spirit duly went to the apsara, who through her own fault was forced to marry him. Despite his bravery,

Bavawala was killed; his queen committed suttee for him and other ladies of the palace were added to the Sultan's harem.

The king of Jetpur was justly punished: he had allowed a fakir in his kingdom to live in danger of starvation; and neither his bravery nor his attempts to help the princess could blot out his original fault nor the workings of destiny ensuing from it.

Everything for the Best

This legend, which shows how through confrontation with the primitive forces of indigenous India a great king came to trust in the divine providence of the orthodox Hindu pantheon, is found with variations in many parts of India. In this version, which originated in Gujarat, the king is said to rule the whole subcontinent. The danger, which sometimes comes from wild animals, comes here from Bhils, an aboriginal hill tribe whose tribal deity is said to be a tigress. In ancient times the Bhils may have worshipped the tigress; in modern times they pay special reverence to Kali, the terrible bloodthirsty form of Shiva's consort, who derives from that aspect of the Dravidian Earth Mother which is based on a deified tiger. Similar tribes, such as the Gonds, are known to have performed fertility sacrifices with human victims; and nowadays the Bhils sacrifice animals twice a year to protect their flocks from tiger attack. The choice of a physically perfect victim was important, and he could belong neither to the Brahmin (priestly) caste, nor to the Kshatriya (warrior or princely) caste. Any mistake might not only make the ceremony of propitiation valueless: it might positively incur the enmity of the slighted deity. This would affect the officiants themselves and the welfare of the whole tribe; and once the balance of man's relationship with his deities was disturbed all manner of calamities could be expected to ensue. Such an attitude to the gods, based on fear and assuming their ill-will, was at variance with the new doctrine illustrated by this legend, according to which man cannot consciously direct or influence his fate, but must put his faith in an ultimately benevolent providence.

In ancient days there was a rich and powerful king who ruled a kingdom that stretched from the Himalayas as far south as Ceylon, and from the Rann of Kutch as far east as the Irrawaddy. Caravan loads brought daily wealth into his capital and his domains and fortune were well administered by his ministers under the guidance of his uncle Pratapsingh who, being only a few years older, was also a close friend. The only irritation the king sometimes suffered was to see the ills of famine, epidemic and wars which men seemed unable to avoid. He could not reconcile this with Pratapsingh's oft-repeated belief that 'everything is for the best'. When challenged, Pratapsingh would reply that such burdens enable man's nature and teach him wisdom, so bringing mankind slowly towards perfection.

One day the king and hid friend went out riding. Hardly had they left the palace when a deer crossed their path from right to left. Pratapsingh advised the king to return, for this was an evil omen; but the king scoffed at such superstition and insisted on pursuing the deer. On and on they rode, until at last the found themselves lost deep in the jungle. While waiting for rescue they set their horses free

to graze and began to look for food and water. At length they discovered a solitary wood apple. The king, hastening to cut it in two with his sword, allowed the apple to slip and cut off his own finger. 'So everything's for the best is it?' asked the king ironically. His mood soon turned to fury when Pratapsingh replied that he believed it must be so; despite his pain and hunger, he took up his sword and ordered Pratapsingh out of his sight.

Seeing that this was no time for conciliation, Pratapsingh did as he was bidden and hid himself at some distance in a thorn bush, the only cover he could find. The king, meanwhile, fell into an uneasy sleep. As he lay at the foot of a tree, he was discovered by Bhil tribesmen who, on the last day of their great annual festival, were seeking a sacrificial victim for their tigress-goddess. They bound up the king and, taking him to their rough mud and stone altar, attached him to a stake in front of the idol, a crudely carved woman whose gaping fanged mouth was smeared with blood. After wild dancing the final sacrificial preparations began with the smearing of red and yellow powder over the victim's forehead, feet and hands. Suddenly a cry went up: the king's missing finger was noticed. The Bhils fled in horror, for they had nearly presented an imperfect sacrifice and feared the wrath of the insulted goddess.

The king realized that the loss of his finger had

indeed been for the best. But what of the bruised and scratched body of Pratapsingh, who by now had searched him out: was that for the best? Yes, said Pratapsingh, for if he had known of the king's peril he would have come to his aid and been overcome by the numerous Bhils, thus serving as a substitute victim. So everything was for the best: the Bhils were rounded up and their cruel idol destroyed; they and all the king's subjects were taught the doctrine of divine providence. By proclamation throughout the kingdom, all were forbidden to doubt Pratapsingh's maxim.

Tales from Central India

The History of Hirde Shah

Hirde Shah was a seventeenth-century hero of the Gond people living in the eastern part of what is today Madhya Pradesh, who built a palace at Ramnagar, near the town of Mandla. As in this legend, his kingdom was subject to the Mogul Empire, and the relations described with the court at Delhi are based on fact. Since the 1570's, when Akbar the Great consolidated the conquests he had made piecemeal throughout northern India, kingdoms subject to Mogul rule had been obliged to pay a single tax of one-third of the produce of the land. This replaced the previous arrangement where by the levy amounted to one-sixth and was augmented by subject kings. The latter also resented Akbar's systematic methods in branding all livestock, especially horses, apportioned for the central government. In the legend, Budhan Shah rebels against this system. But Hirde Shah was in fact the son of Prem Narayan, who was treacherously killed by Jhujhar Singh, and it was Jhujhar Singh, not Aurangzeb, against whom he fought. The issue of religion was paramount in Mogul India and it came to a head during the reign of Aurangzeb from 1658 to 1707 A.D. Unlike Akbar, who had encouraged free discussion of religious matters and permitted diverse faiths to co-exist, Aurangzeb was a fanatic. In A.D. 1669 he prohibited the Hindu religion and began the destruction of Hindu temples. This was followed in 1679 by a tax on all non-Moslems; in imposing harsh financial penalties, Aurangzeb largely ignored the poverty of his subject peoples. In everyday life, too, he tried to impose his will. His grandfather Jehangir had allowed power to slip from his hands through addiction to drink; Aurangzeb's disapproval of alcohol, opium and tobacco was fierce. Yet though he maintained the largest army in the whole of the

contemporary world (200,000, not the five Million of the legend), his intolerance produced the first effective reaction against mogul rule. Historically, the Mahratta leader Sivaji Bhonsle was the greatest thorn in his flesh. Aurangzeb was thus the natural opponent for the Gond hero. Aurangzeb's son Akbar, who in the legend tried to force his sister to remain a Moslem, in fact rebelled against his father's harsh intolerance and after refusing to attempt suppression of the Rajputs, took refuge with the Mahrattas of the Deccan. In this legend the hated Moguls take the place of the rakshasas of traditional legends. The heroes flaunt their non-Moslem practices, perform impossible tasks, and triumph. In the Gond country the kingdom of Godbanka was ruled by Lodha Sardar and the kingdom of Garha by his brother Budhan Shah. Budhan Shah, who was known as a great drunkard, had three wives and a son called Hirde Shah. He had been given the kingdom by Aurangzeb, to whom be had to pay tribute; but as the country was nothing but wild jungle, it amounted to very little; fifty pounds each of wild rice; figs and honey, together with some jungle fruit, such as bel-fruit, a fruit associated with Shiva. Budhan was a devotee of Shiva — for he was said to seek intoxication also — and of his consort Devi, the Great Mother.

After some Aurangzeb became impatient with the paltry tribute he received and ordered one of his ministers to spy out the land the in Garha. But the minister refused to go, fearing that he would be insulted by the raja. Instead, an opium-eating fakir was sent. According to his custom, and in order not to arouse suspicion, the fakir travelled about Budhan's city on his donkey, begging for holy alms. To his astonishment, he collected fifty pounds of the palace was so big that it took twelve buffaloes to open it. The fakir stood at these gates and asked that his arrival should be reported to the raja. The palace sentry would have killed him for his insolence, but Budhan Shah ordered that the fakir should be well received, and given food in the palace.

After three months the fakir said farewell and secretly prepared to return to Delhi. Budhan Shah presented him with parting gifts of a horse and a carpet, and asked him to name as a third gift whatever he wished. To test the raja's sincerity, the fakir asked him to spit on the ground. This Budhan did; but he angrily refused when the fakir then asked him to lick up his spittle. The fakir therefore asked instead for Budhan's ceremonial shoes — decorated golden shoes which were a symbol of his royal power. The members of Budhan's court were horrified at such a request, but Budhan had promised to grant whatever the fakir requested, and was bound by his promise. When Aurangzeb heard the fakir's account of the munificence of the alms in Garha and saw the golden shoes, he sent a message to Budhan Shah demanding a golden grindstone and the elephant Bhaoranand and threatening that if Budhan refused he would lose his kingdom. Budhan, however, had Aurangzeb's messengers beaten and sent back to Delhi with the message that Aurangzeb would have to conquer him.

As soon as he received Budhan's answer, Aurangzeb set off from Delhi with his army of five million to attack Garha. Soon the Mogul army could be seen surrounding Budhan's city on all sides. Budhan was fearful for his three wives, so he ordered his minister to dress as a mahout and his wives as male ascetics and sent them out of the city on an elephant. So huge was the surrounding enemy encampment that it took them three days to pass through it. On the third day, suspicions were aroused, and the ranis prayed to Mother Earth to save them. At once a great storm arose and a flood which killed thousands of Pathan soldiers. Ranis and elephant became invisible and escaped.

Meanwhile within the palace all were convinced that Aurangzeb would seek nothing less than to wipe out the Gondi religion and to enforce Islam. Budhan Shah, looking at the size of the enemy force, saw no hope. His son Hirde Shah, however, would not so easily admit defeat. Though only twelve years old, as soon as he knew his mothers to be safe he begged his father for permission to start killing Moslems. At last Budhan Shah agreed, and Hirde Shah climbed to the topmost part of the palace to look at the Mogul army. But Budhan Shah, preferring to die by his own hand, stabbed himself. When Hirde Shah saw his father dead he set up such piercing lamentations that Aurangzeb himself could hear the weeping. The Great Mogul sent his spies to find out the cause. As soon as they had reported, Aurangezb attacked and took the city and threw the boy Hirde into prison. In prison, Hirde remembered his uncle Lodha Sardar and wrote him a letter, which flew through the air to reach him at his court in Godbanka.

Angry at his brother's fate, Lodha at once set off alone for Garha, mounted on his horse Grudbaj. Fortifying himself with alcohol as he rode, Lodha soon reached the Pathan soldiers surrounding the city. While his horse kicked all about him,

Lodha Sardar alone killed hundreds, piling up their headless bodies and creating a river of blood. Then one Pathan, pretending to be dead, succeeded in cutting off Grudbaj's legs. Lodha thereupon took to his feet and began to drink Pathan blood. Thus strengthened, he dropped his weapons and kicked all but a dozen to death. These, however, captured him in a surprise attack, and the battle was over. Hirde Shah was now put in a chariot to be taken to Delhi. Seeing this, Lodha begged to be killed. Three times the Pathans struck off Lodhas head, but three times it joined up again to his body. At last they split his body from end to end and he died. Then they threw his body into a lake, where it turned the water black and killed all the lake's inhabitants. With Lodha Sardar dead, Hirde Shah was treated as a common prisoner in Delhi. He was given nothing but water and gram to eat, but even this he refused. When he had lived thus for six months without food, Aurangzeb began to fear his power. He therefore set him an impossible task on pain of death: to break a stone with a crumbling lump of *ganja*, an intoxicant; but Hirde Shah broke the stone. Then they threw him down a well with a stone round his neck; but Hirde escaped unhurt.

Hirde Shah used to live by the well, where he was seen by the womenfolk. When they told Aurangzeb's daughter of his beauty, she had an underground passage made to the well and came to see him. She dressed as a Hindu, for she feared he would despise a Moselm girl, and she told him she would throw over Islam and become a Gond for love of him. At first Hirde would have nothing to do with her; but after some time he was persuaded share with her a feast of pork. Thus they lived together secretly in the palace.

After a month, however, they were found out by Aurangzeb's son Akbar. They ran away to Ramnagar, where Hirde built a great fort. Aurangzeb sent his army of five million to punish Hirde Shah and his daughter; but when they came to Ramnagar the princess turned them away with a Moslem oath. Hirde Shah became a great and rich king. After his death he became immortal and invisible.

Singhisurwa and Palibirwa

Singhisurwa is a legendary hero of the Gonds. He is sometimes treated as a king, sometimes as a giant, and sometimes as the leader of the Singhi, supernatural beings who help the Gond kings in Battle. There is a fort at Chanda, in Berar. This legend includes the common motif of the hero who protects an animal's offsping and is rewarded with help in performing the impossible task which proves his superhuman stature. The idea of reincarnation facilitates the notion that animals play a part in human destiny , and regard for them is a sign of heroic nobility.

Bhogibila Singh Raja was a wealthy and fearless king who lived in the seven-storey fort at Chanda, alone except for his family and his army. For twenty-four years he received no visitor. His fort was surrounded by traps, and each gate was guarded by twelve soldiers.

One day Singhisurwa, king of Palinagri, rode to Chanda on his mammoth horse Hansdhar to ask for the hand of Bhogibila's daughter Gaila on behalf of his five-year-old son Palibirwa. When he arrived at Chanda after his long journey, he encamped in Bhogibila's flower garden, which was visible from the fort. Here he pitched his tent, fastening it with twelve golden pegs, and prepared to rest. While he slept, his horse Hansdhar began to trample the flowers like an elephant. Bhogibila saw this and sent his servants to seize Singhisurwa. But Singhisurwa, who slept with one eye and one ear always open, was prepared. He sent word to Bhogibila telling why he had come. But Bhogibila scorned the kings of Palinagri and was the more incensed. He ordered his troops to prepare for battle. Meanwhile, Singhisurwa slept on, for eight days and nine

nights. At the end of this long sleep his preparations were complete; rest had restored all his powers, and he had summoned to him the spirits of the unseen world: Mother Earth and Vasuki the serpent upholder of the earth; also Fire, Whirlwind, she-devils, hornets and the spirits of the night. This army killed half the Chanda soldiers on its own; still Singhisurwa slept on. Then Hansdhar kicked him awake and bore Singhisurwa like an arrow into the middle of the battle. Singhisurwa and his supernatural helpers killed the entire Chanda army, until at last the fight was reduced to single combat between the two kings. For eight days and nine nights they fought until at last Singhisurwa was pushed off his horse and into a secret pit used as an armoury. Bhogibila made haste to lock his enemy in; but Hansdhar would not admit his master's defeat and carried on the fight by kicking all about him. When his hooves had shattered everything in view, Hansdhar set off home to Palinagri.

Becoming thirsty on the way, he stopped to drink

by a well in the forest. The well was surrounded by snares and guarded by a sword hanging above it which clanged when anyone approached. As Hansdhar drank his fiil, the sword gave its warning, but when the king who owned the well and his court tried to catch him, Hansdhar bit them and kicked them mightily, and then rose in the air and flew to Palinagri.

Hansdhar told the weeping rani that her husband was dead, killed by the treachery of Bhogibila. Her little son Palibirwa also listened to the story and, immediately making oblations to Mother Earth, jumped on to Hansdhar's back and flew off with him to see what had happened to Singhisurwa. On their way to Chanda, they came across the nest of the vulture queen Gidhal. In it were twelve nestlings; but ten were dead, killed by a cobra, which was just about to strike the remaining two.

Taking the horse's advice, Paliibirwa struck the cobra dead and cut it into pieces. When Gidhal returned, her

children told her how Palibirwa had saved their lives, and she gave the boy her blessing, telling him he might call on her help when he was in trouble. When Palibirwa arrived at Chanda he pitched his sumptuous golden tent before the fort and there spread his golden mattress and silken bedding on his gold and pearl bedstead. The sight astonished Bhogibila and the thirtysix kings, twenty-one princes and the wealthy citizens of fifty-two towns who were gathered in the fort for a durbar to do homage to their overlord Bhogibila.

Rising early next morning, Palibirwa opened the war by getting Hansdhar to destroy Bhogibila's garden. Then, having polluted Bhogibila's well, whose bathing slab was made of gold, he picked up the slab and broke it with such force that a splinter was hurled at the king's elephant and killed it. After this, Palibirwa threw the rest of the slab into the midst of the durbar, killing half the assembly. Fierce battle was joined and the slaughter created a river of blood. Wild animals came rushing from the jungle to devour the dead. But at last Palibirwa killed and beheaded Bhogibila. Then, seizing the queen by the hair, he demanded to know where his father was; but she did not know. Eventually, Palibirwa found his father in the pit, still firmly impaled on the spears stored in it.

Calling on Mother Earth, Palibirwa rescued his father and restored him to life. Then they set off home on Hansdhar's back, carrying with them the head of Bhogibila and the baby Gaila as a bride for Palibirwa. As they flew over the jungle tribes, Palibirwa shouted out his triumph; and on their return he became king.

Tales from Northern India

Raja Rasalu

Raja Rasalu is the greatest legendary figure of the Punjab. He is described as the son of Salivahana (Salbahan), who overthrew the empire of Vikramaditya and founded the Scythian era in A.D. 78. In fact he was probably an Indo-Scythian hero some time between A.D. 300 and 900. Atak, the kingdom of Raja Hodi, his rival in love, extended from the Indus through the Peshawar valley to beyond the Khyber Pass in the third century A.D. His other great enemy, Raja Sarkap or Sirikap, also had Afghan association: Mount Gandgarh, not far from the ancient site of Taxila, where he lived and was said to have built his fort of men's skulls, is still inhabited by descendants of Afghan intruders. In the Rasalu legend Mount Gandgarh, which is subject to earthquakes that cause roaring in its caves, is also the home of the rakshasas; these giants or monsters usually represent the indigenous peoples of India, subjugated by the invading Aryans but still feared by them.

Though historically Rasalu was not an Aryan, his legend in this respect ascribes conventional Aryan prowess to him. Indeed his name has been connected with story cycles embodying almost every motif of Indian legend. The Punjab being an area where Hinduism and Islam were strongly interpenetrated, each community vied to claim Rasalu as its own and to emphasize the hero's choice in the conflict of the two faiths. Thus, according to the faith of bard and audience, Raja Rasalu is a good Hindu or, like Guru Gugga, is converted to Islam. Moslem accounts of the hero tell how his exile following the repudiation of the bride chosen by his father led to a dramatic conversion to Islam; it culminated in his defeat of his father and conquest of his patrimony, Sialkot, partly in retaliation for his father's sacrifice of a Moslem boy-a rite intended to strengthen the fortifications of Sialkot.

Most probably, however, Rasalu was himself an

opponent of the Moslem invaders, Hajjaj and Muhammed Qasim, between A.D. 697 and 713. A greater proportion of the legends told by the Hindu bards seem to belong to Rasalu alone and to have a greater link with historical events - even if they do include prime examples of the stock motifs. It is chiefly the Hindu legends that concern us here.

Raja Salbahan, who in ancient times ruled at Sialkot in Lahore, had two queens. The elder, Achhra, had borne him a fine son called Puran. The younger, Rani Lona, was a creature of unrivalled beauty and grace for, unknown to Salbahan, she was an apsara or fairy, one of the dancing girls of Indra's heaven. Lona fell in love with her stepson Puran, who was the same age as herself, and tried to seduce him. The virtuous Puran, however, rejected her advances; wherein she revenged herself by complaining to Salbahan of Puran's infamous behaviour to her. The father, believing all his beautiful wife

told to him, had Puran's hands and feet cut off, and then had him thrown into a deep well. Somehow Puran managed to stay alive at the bottom of the well for a long time, until one day Guru Gorakhnath passed that way, discovered Puran still alive and through hie prayers restored his hands and feet to him. He then began to teach Puran, who became his most illustrious disciple.

After a while Gorakhnath allowed Puran to revisit Sialkot. He did not at first announce his presence to his parents, but went to live in the palace garden, where he had played as a boy. But he found the garden sadly changed: it was parched and neglected, as befitted a household where happiness was now unknown. Puran's mother had become blind from weeping over his fate, while Salbahan and Lona grieved over their failure to have a son. Puran prayed that the garden might become green again, and immediately every tree and plant sprouted fresh leaves. The miraculous powers of the holy man were spoken of far and wide, and when his reputation reached the palace Rani Achhra visited him in the garden, hoping to be cured of her blindness. Puran did not reveal to her that he was her son, but through his prayers restored her sight. Salbahan and Lona, learning of this, made haste to visit the guru and beg him for a son. 'But Raja Salbahan has a son already', said Puran. 'Where is he?' And so in Salbahan's presence, he forced Lona to tell the true story; so great was her longing for a son that she would do even this. Puran then revealed his identity; but he was pleased that Lona had told the truth and gave her a magic grain of rice, telling her that when she ate it she would become pregnant. He added, however, the though the son she would bear would be brave and holy, he would leave her and cause such grief that she would weep even more than Achhra had done. On learning of this dubious blessing, Lona paused.

Conscious of her past cruelty to Achhra, she trembled at the thought of expiating it with greater torments. But such was her longing for a son and her wish to provide Salbahan with an heir that she took the grain of rice and conceived. As for Puran, he had long since renounced the world, and departed once more from Sialkot to serve his master Gorakhnath.

Shortly before the birth her child, astrologers foretold that the child would become a great man who should be called Rasalu; but that if either his father or his mother were to see him during the twelve years after his birth they would die instantly. They advised that the infant should be confined to a cellar for twelve years. Accordingly when Lona sent word from her palace that a son had been born, Salbahan ordered that he should be shut away in a underground palace, where he would be looked after by a number of nurses who would teach him the princely arts. For companionship a colt, Bhaunr Iraqi, born on the same day as Rasalu, and a parrot, both of whom could talk, were also shut into the underground palace; and a sword, spear and shield were placed ready for Rasalu's first appearance in the light of day in twelve year's time.

At first Rasalu grew up contentedly; but his was not a nature to bear confinement, and at the end of eleven years, when he had learnt all he could from his guardians, he insisted, despite their protests, on riding forth into the world, wearing his armour and accompanied by his parrot. His faithful horse bore him thus arrayed into his father's city of Sialkot. He announced his presence forthwith by throwing stones at the earthen pitchers of the women drawing water from the well by the city gates and breaking them all. When the women went to complain to Salbahan, the raja guessed that the miscreant was his son, and gave them brass pitchers. But Rasalu's iron-tipped arrows pierced these too. Still Salbahan refused to summon the boy, who therefore burst into his audience chamber; but the raja, knowing that he risked his won life if he looked on Rasalu before another year had passed, turned his back on his son. Rasalu, spurned apparently by his own father, decided to seek his fortune elsewhere and set out on Bhaunr Iraqi, accompanied by his parrot, a carpenter and a goldsmith. As Rasalu left Sialkot he received the blessing of his mother, whom he could not see but heard weeping from her tower window.

The very first night, having reached a part of the jungle far from any human habitation, Rasalu and his companions prepared to sleep, dividing the night into three watches. The carpenter lad took the first watch, and while the others were asleep a serpent came out and made as if to attack them. 'Who are you', asked the carpenter, 'and what do you want?' 'I have slain every being for twelve miles around:

how dare you come here', answered the serpent. But the brave carpenter fought the serpent and killed him, hiding the body under his shield lest Rasalu, unused to the perils of the outside world, should be frightened. But when the third watch came and Rasalu stood guard, a great monster emerged from the jungle, telling Rasalu that it had slain every being for forty-eight miles about. A dreadful struggle ensued, but Rasalu chased the monster to a cave and there slew it. In the morning the carpenter proudly showed his companions the dead serpent; but Rasalu said, 'That is only a little snake; come and see what I killed.' His companions saw the fearsome corpse and were horror-struck. They realized that Rasalu, though only eleven, was a hero and attracted heroic opponents; but they were not made to face such perils. They therefore said farewell and returned to the city, leaving Rasalu with his horse and parrot, and determined to pursue his destiny, for a king must act as a king. Thereafter Rasalu had many adventures, during which he proved his valour and grew in wisdom. Among the legendary rulers whom he encountered were Mirshikari, the hunter king, who ensnared animals by going into the forest and playing the flute to lure them. Rasalu advised Mirshikari that he would be safe from all harm while hunting to the north, to the east and to the west, but that he must always avoid hunting in the southern part of the forest. Mirshikari, however, ignored this advice, and died as a result. After this Rasalu journeyed on into the kingdom of Raja Bhoj and became his adviser. With Rasalu's aid, Raja Bhoj learned to act as a wise judge. Rasalu thus soon proved his skills of judgement and foresight as a ruler, even though exiled from his own kingdom. Also he was once more to demonstrate his courage and prowess at arms. After some years he came to Nila, a strangely deserted city, where he found an old woman making bread and weeping as she worked. She explained to him that Nila and its inhabitants lived under constant threat of annihilation by the rakshasas or giant ogres who lived at the foot of nearby Mount Gandgarh. The hunger of these rakshasas could be appeased only by daily tribute of a bullock, all the bread he could carry on his back, and one young man. The old woman had already lost six sons thus, and that day her seventh and last son had been selected as the victim. Rasalu told her not to weep, for he had come and would take her son's place.

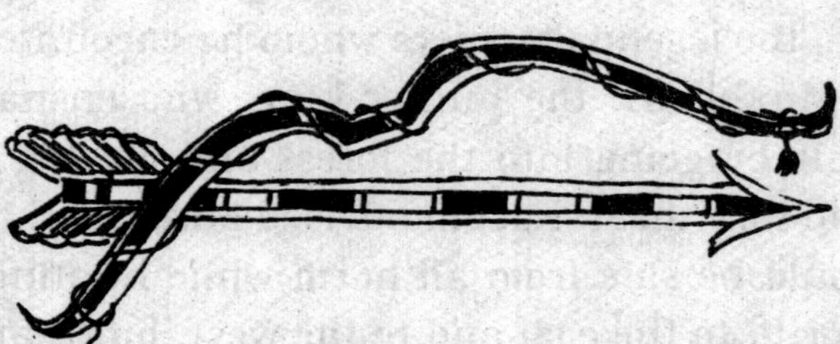

The old woman could hardly believe this until she learnt that this was Rasalu, for legend had it that one day a raja called Rasalu would rid the city of the race of rakshasas.

Next morning Rasalu set off for the rakshasa country, riding Bhaunr Iraqi and carrying his parrot on his arm: both would give him good advice in the coming struggle. Before him he drove the bullock laden with bread. No sooner had they entered rakshasa territory than one of these monsters appeared before them. So big was he that at first Rasalu thought he was a mountain, but soon the grisly features could be distinguished: the matted hair and bloodstained teeth, the large belly, legs like tree trunks, the five feet, and fingers set backwards. This rakshasa, who was carrying a water skin made of the hides of twenty-seven buffaloes, hurried forward eagerly towards Rasalu, for he saw that in addition to the usual tribute there was a horse, and he hoped to devour it himself before his brothers saw it. As he raised his hand to the horse, however, Rasalu brought down his sword and with a stroke cut off his massive arm. His loud and terrible cries shook the earth and brought his sister running; when she saw what had happened she fled in terror, knowing in her heart that Raja Rasalu was at hand.

Panic spread among the rakshasas as their astrologer brother consulted his books and confirmed that Raja Rasalu, their predestined destroyer, had been born into the world. But Rasalu pursued and cornered them. One of the bravest thought to challenge him: if he were the real Rasalu his heel ropes would be able to bind them and his sword cut them up on its own. So Rasalu loosened his heel ropes and dropped his sword to the ground; and the ropes bound a rakshasa immobile until the sword had hacked him to pieces, and so on one after the other until the sword had hacked him to pieces, and so on one after the other until only seven rakshasas were left, together with one rakshasi, their sister.

The seven rakshasas challenged Rasalu once again to prove his identity. They said that it had been foretold that Rasalu would be able to pierce seven griddles, each one weighing thirty-five tons, set one behind the other. Rasalu, accepting the challenge, loosened one of his iron arrows, which transfixed not only the griddles but also the seven rakshasas, who were lined up behind them.

There now remained only the rakshasi; but she, thinking herself wilier than her brothers, had escaped and hidden in a cave. Here Raja Rasalu found her out; but on the advice of the horse and parrot he did not venture into the recesses of the mountain. He rolled a great stone in front of the cave, and beside it placed a great image of himself in armour; its shadow falling across the entrance to the cave so frightened the rakshasi that she dared not attempt escape. To this day she can be heard giving vent to her fury, for the whole mountain shakes when she breathes hard.

Rasalu then journeyed on to seek more adventure. When he came to Hodinagari, the city of Raja Harichand (which was probably on the Indus in Rawalpindi), he approached the palace of Rani Sundran, Harichand's daughter, whose beauty was famed throughout the land. At her gate he found an old yogi, who told him that he had been sitting there by his sacred fire for twenty-two years in the hope of catching a glimpse of her fabled beauty. The yogi had heard of Rasalu and was surprised when the hero asked him to make him his disciple. Why should he become a yogi when as an apsara's son he could already perform miracles? But he agreed and pierced Rasalu's ears for the sacred earrings and gave him a yogi's loincloth. Then the two sat together outside the palace. For two days the yogi begged and shared his food with Rasalu; but while Rasalu was holy and did not need food, the yogi felt starved. He therefore told Rasalu to beg.

Rasalu sang a song to Sundran outside the gate, begging for alms; and Sundran heard him from within and was moved by his sweet voice. She sent out a maid with alms; but when the maid beheld the handsome beggar she was so overcome that she fainted away, dropping the alms. The same happened again with a second maid. Rasalu sang his song for a third time, and now Sundran herself came to the gate and, putting the food aside, filled the plate with jewels. Then, presenting them to Rasalu, she asked him how long he had been a yogi and what he wanted of her. Rasalu replied that he had been a yogi only one day and sought alms from no one but fair Sundran; then he returned to his master. But the yogi was not content with Sundran's munificence, for how could he eat jewels? He sent Rasalu back with the jewels to ask for food instead. Sundran, declaring her love for him, sent for food, but not until it was ready would Rasalu speak. Then he revealed his name and said he had become a yogi only to see if her reputation for beauty was justified; having seen her he would now depart for ever. He took the food to the yogi and then pursued his way. Sundran nevertheless waited to hear his song again; and when she heard nothing, went outside the palace gates for the first time to seek out the yogi. The yogi's wish to see her was thus fulfilled after twenty-two years; but he was angry that after all his devotion, she should come only to ask for a stranger, and told her roughly that he had roasted Rasalu and eaten him because he had not brought enough alms. 'Then roast and eat me too', said Sundran, throwing herself on the yogi's fire for love of Rasalu.

Rasalu, however, gave no further thought to Sundran. After a while he decided that he would like to try the experience of reigning as a king, so he seized the throne of Sundran's father Harichand and reigned for some years at Hodinagari. But before long adventure beckoned once more. Rasalu heard of the mysterious Raja Sarkap, 'Be-header', whose delight was to play a dice game, chaupur, with his guests. Sarkap played for high stakes and as he used enchanted dice no opponent had ever beaten him; each had paid with his head. Rasalu, however, resolved to play chaupur with Sarkap.

As he journeyed towards Sarkap's city, Rasalu was overtaken by a violent storm and took refuge in a graveyard. Here a headless corpse spoke to him and, hearing of Rasalu's mission, revealed that he was Sarsuk, Sarkap's brother, who himself had lost his head after a game of chaupur with the raja. Sarsuk advised Rasalu that his only hope lay in playing with dice made of bones from the graveyard. So before setting out next morning Rasalu fashioned some dice from the bones scattered about and put them in his pocket.

As he rode on, Rasalu passed a forest fire out of which he heard a voice. It was only that of a cricket, but the kindhearted hero snatched it from the fire; in gratitude, the cricket gave Rasalu one of its feelers, telling him that he had only to drop it on a fire when he was in difficulties and the cricket

would come to his aid. Rasalu hardly believed he could ever need a cricket's aid, but took the feeler. At last Rasalu entered the garden of Sarkap's palace. Here he saw Sarkap's seventy daughters. All were gay except the youngest who, struck by the handsome stranger, warned him not to play chaupur with her father, for he would surely lose he head. Rasalu, however, was not to be dissuaded: he assured the girl he would not lose and promised to marry her. At this her sixty-nine sisters became jealous and warned Rasalu that he must perform a task set by them if he wished to become their younger brother. Rasalu readily agreed, so they mixed eighty pounds of millet with eighty pounds of sand and ordered him to sort them out again. When they had gone Rasalu took the cricket's feeler and put it on a fire; immediately a swarm of crickets flew to him and in a flash had sorted the grain.

Next morning the astonished girls set Rasalu another task: he should push each of them on a swing one after the other until they were tired. Rasalu saw that seventy girls in rotation would never become tired, but they accepted his offer to push them all at once. When they had all climbed on to one swing he sent it flying with his bow; but on its return he cut the rope with his sword so that all the girls tumbled to the ground, and all were hurt except the youngest.

Then Rasalu strode over the seventy gongs and

seventy drums which were set up in the garden to summon Sarkap to chaupur. Striking them with his mighty arm, he shattered them all. At this the youngest daughter ran to warn her father of Rasalu's prowess. Sarkap had heard of Rasalu and was afraid; but he spoke defiantly and sent food to the house where Rasalu was resting until the hour for chaupur. Rasalu, however, would not take gifts from an enemy and threw the food to Sarkap's dog. Instantly, the dog dropped dead, for the food was poisoned. The servants were angrily sent back to tell Sarkap of Rasalu's disdain for an enemy who would use treachery.

At last the hour for chaupur arrived. As Rasalu, fully armed, rode to the palace gates on Bhaunr Iraqi, he sow a cat running about near a kiln. Asking her what was wrong, he learned that her kittens were trapped in a pot that was about to be fired. So Rasalu bought the entire kiln from the potter and rescued the kittens. The mother cat in gratitude insisted that he take one of the kittens, for it would help him when he was in difficulties; so Rasalu slipped the kitten into his pocket and rode on.

The contest began with riddles, but Rasalu could answer them all. Then the chaupur board was brought forth and the stakes were fixed. On the first game Sarkap wagered his kingdom, on the second the wealth of the whole world, and on the third his head. Raja Rasalu wagered his arms on the first game, his horse on the second, and his head on the third. Play began, but Rasalu had forgotten Sarsuk's warning and used Sarkap's dice; furthermore Sarkap released his rat Dhol Raja, who ran over the board upsetting the pieces. Thus Rasalu lost the first game and his hand in his arms, the second game and his horse. As Bhaunr Iraqi was taken away he spoke to his master, reminding him to -put his hand in his pocket. Rasalu regained his confidence and insisted on using his own dice; and he sent the kitten to guard the rat hole from which Dhol Raja had run out during the first two games. At this Sarkap ordered all the womenfolk of the palace to put on their finery and crowd round to distract Rasalu. But Rasalu never glanced at them, and as play continued he won back his horse and arms and then, in two more games, Sarkap's kingdom and the wealth of the world.

Then, as the seventh game was ended and Sarkap forfeited his head, a servant entered to announce the birth of a daughter to Sarkap. The defeated raja cursed her and ordered her to be killed instantly, for she had been born in an evil hour. But Rasalu, magnanimous in victory, told Sarkap to spare her life, just as he would spare Sarkap's provided he would promise never again to play chaupur for another's head. Sarkap agreed, and presented the baby to Rasalu together with a mango branch. The beautiful infant, who was named Kokilan, was placed in an underground palace outside which Rasalu planted the mango branch. When the mango flowered in twelve years' time, Rasalu promised, he would return and marry Kokilan.

Twelve years later he bore his bride off to his palace hidden deep in the jungle, where every day he would go hunting. One day Kokilan, curious to know how Rasalu hunted, went with him into the forest. After watching him, however, she demonstrated that she could catch a deer without the benefit of weapons. Sitting on the ground, she spread her scented hair and attracted to her two deer, Hira and Nila. Rasalu frightened Nila away with his bow, but Hira remained. Seeing how fond Hira was of his wife, Rasalu wanted to make sure he would never kill him and so marked him by cutting off his tail and ears before releasing him. But his disfigurement made Hira an outcast from the herd and he vowed revenge, saying, 'I will bring a thief into your garden.'

Hira therefore went into the kingdom of Raja Hodi and there destroyed Hodi's garden. Seeing the destruction, Hodi gave chase; the deer lured him on hour after hour until they reached Rasalu's palace and then, having explained that he acted on the orders of Kokilan, pointed her out at the window. Rasalu had as usual gone off hunting for the day, leaving Kokilan alone except for the company of his parrot and a myna bird, who watched over her. Kokilan and Hodi fell in love at the sight of each other and lost no time in declaring their passion. Kokilan let down a rope from her window and Hodi climbed up to her chamber. The two birds, her guardians, commented on her shameless behaviour, and the myna bird chided her for her infidelity. But the parrot, not such a foolish

friend, silenced the myna bird. The lovers parted just before Rasalu's return, but not before Hodi had drawn water from the well and broken its brim.

When Rasalu saw the broken well and the disorder in the palace, he asked who had been there. Kokilan replied that she herself had drawn the heavy bucket of water and that the birds had created the disarray by attacking her. Rasalu punished the birds and then once more went off hunting. Soon Hodi returned and this time the myna bird could not be prevented from voicing his protest and was killed by Kokilan. The parrot saved his own life by praising Kokilan for her action, and so mollified her that she let him out of his cage 'so that he could kick the disloyal myna bird'. No sooner had he gained his freedom, however, than the parrot flew up to the palace roof, where he began to weep loudly over the fate of the foolish myna. Kokilan realized that she had been duped by the parrot, but no threats or cajoling from her could coax him back. The faithful parrot then flew off into the jungle to inform Rasalu of Kokilan's treachery.

Rasalu hurried back to his palace bearing two spits, one already full of game, the other still empty. Reaching the palace, he saw Raja Hodi leaving it. As Hodi stood at the top of a flight of sixty steps, Rasalu challenged him. At first Hodi feigned innocence. He tried to pretend he did not know whose palace it was, and said he had strayed there after losing himself in the jungle. But Rasalu poured scorn on him for resorting to subterfuge: such cowardice was unworthy of a king. He commanded him to acknowledge his actions and fight in his own defence as a king should. Knowing that he was in the wrong and besides fearing Rasalu's skill, Hodi refused to accept Rasalu's challenge to a duel in which the opponents would take alternate shots; but Rasalu insisted, telling him to have the first shot. So Hodi descended thirty steps and shot the first arrow, but Rasalu parried and cut it in two with his sword. Immediately Hodi prepared to shoot another arrow, despite Rasalu's protests that they had arranged to shoot alternately. But the second arrow too Rasalu parried with his shield. Then Hodi prepared to loose his third arrow, but his bow broke. At this he called for mercy, for he was disarmed. Rasalu said he would shoot one arrow only, and with his one arrow unerringly killed the man who had dishonoured him.

Then, cutting out Hodi's heart, Rasalu put it on his spit and entered the palace. Lulling Kokilan with sweet words, he prepared for her a 'love feast'. Deceived, she ate the heart with enjoyment. 'Why should you not relish his flesh who enjoyed you?' replied Rasalu; whereupon in horror and mortification Kokilan ran to the topmost tower of the palace and threw herself down. Sorrowing, Raja Rasalu picked up the mortally wounded body of his queen, cursed from birth; and strapping her and the body of Hodi to his rival's horse, sent them back to Hodi's kingdom.

Hodi's brothers, when they saw his body, discovered the story and besieged Raja Rasalu in his palace. The mighty hero was ultimately laid low and his head borne off to Hodi's palace.

Raja Harichand, the Upright King

The classical histories name Harichand as the twenty-eighth king of the earliest dynasty in India, the solar race, who reigned at Ayodhya, the capital of Kosala, now Oudh. He was renowned for his piety and just rule. His fate is celebrated in folk legend but is also related in the classical epics. The *Mahabharata* and *Markandeya Purana*, where he is known as Harischandra, tell how he had no son, and to get one vowed to Varuna that he would ultimately sacrifice the son to him. In fact, after many delays, Harischandra's nerve failed and he bought another boy and sacrificed him instead. Despite this, Harischandra was eventually rewarded for his munificent charity with a place in heaven, however, the sage Narada induced him to boast of his merits, for which he was expelled. As he was descending to earth, Harischandra repented of his pride, so his descent was stopped. That is why Harischandra's city can still be seen floating in mid-air, halfway between heaven and earth.

The sage Visvamitra in the following legend was one of the seven great rishis. He himself had also been a Kshatriya and a king, but by dint of his austerities had forced Brahma to grant the impossible: his entry into the Brahmin caste.

Raja Harichand was a great and virtuous king reigning at Ayodhya. He had an only son called

Manikchand of whom he was very proud. Harichand's kingdom was everywhere prosperous and orderly, but above all else the king cherished his garden, the garden of his virtue, in which flowers and fruits in plenty flourished. Harichand neglected no duty, and indeed exceeded what was required, for everyday on rising he would give two and a half pounds of pure gold to some fakir or religious mendicant. Such was the intensity of the raja's virtue that Indra himself became uncomfortable on his throne and decided to send the sage Visvamitra to see if he could destroy Harichand's holiness. Visvamitra therefore descended to earth and, taking the shape of a boar, rampaged through Harichand's garden rooting up every plant. Then he ran off into the jungle. Next morning the gardener called Harichand and showed the king the devastation. Sorrowful as he was, Harichand did not neglect his customary alms giving, and after it he went hunting in the jungle. There he passed Visvamitra, who had now disguised himself as a fakir and begged from

him. Harichand told him that if he would come back to the palace with him he would give him two and a half pounds of gold. 'That cannot be', said the fakir, 'no one would give so much.' But Harichand assured him that he would and bade the fakir follow him. When they reached the palace Harichand sent the treasurer to bring the promised gold; but the treasurer found that all the great raja's gold, silver and jewels had been turned into charcoal. Great was his dismay and that of Harichand, whose name would be dishonoured if he could not keep his promise to the fakir. In order to keep that promise, Harichand told the fakir, he would sell his son, his wife Rani Hirali and himself into service.

He sold Hirali first: she became the servant of a courtesan, Ganga, who paid one pound of gold for her. Then Harichand took his son to a merchant, who paid half a pound of gold for his services. Finally, Harichand sold himself for one pound of gold, and gave all the money to the fakir. For Harichand was reserved the worst humiliation, since his master was an untouchable who tended a funeral pyre. His master explained to him that his task would be to receive the bodies of the dead and throw them on to the pyre. For a man or a woman he would take one rupee and for a child half a rupee; if the relatives had no money Harichand was instructed to take a piece of cloth. Now it happened that Manikchand's master was a good man, and

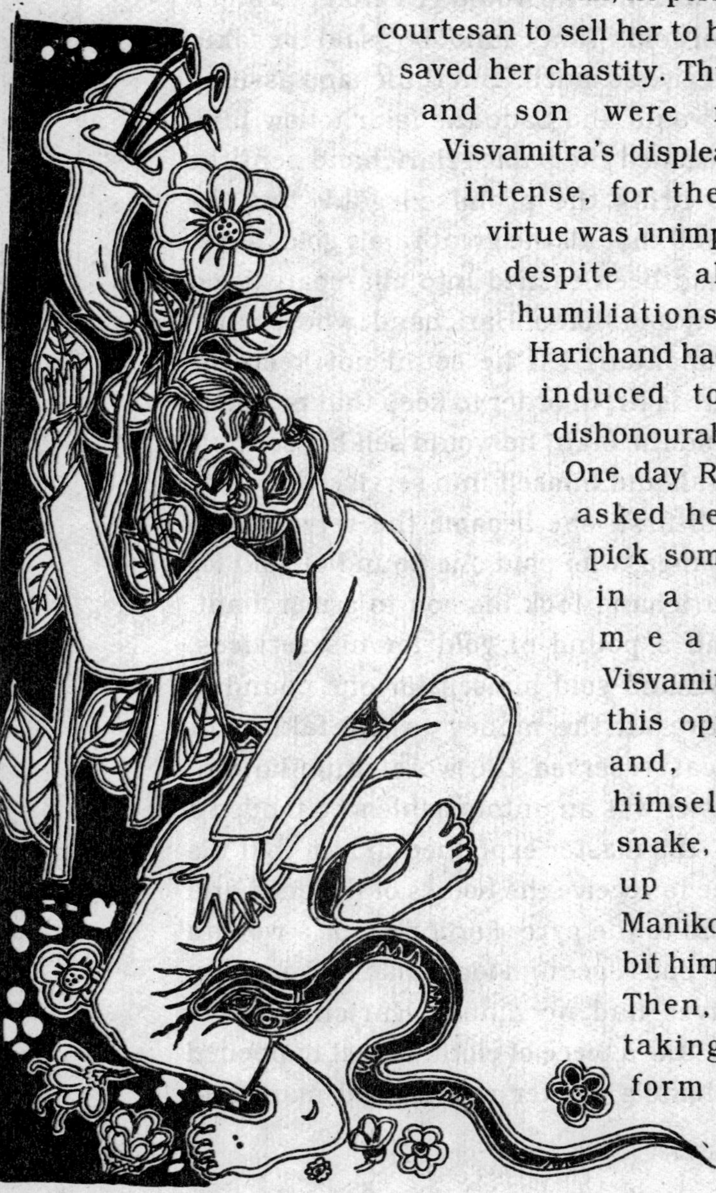

when he heard that the queen had been sold to a courtesan, he persuaded the courtesan to sell her to him and so saved her chastity. Thus mother and son were reunited. Visvamitra's displeasure was intense, for the queen's virtue was unimpaired and despite all his humiliations Raja Harichand had not been induced to behave dishonourably.

One day Rani Hirali asked her son to pick some flowers in a riverside meadow. Visvamitra seized this opportunity and, turning himself into a snake, slithered up to Manikchand and bit him to death. Then, again taking human form as a

Brahmin, Visvamitra told Hirali that her husband was the keeper of the funeral pyre. She therefore took him the body of their son, naturally expecting not to have to pay. But Harichand, overcome as he was with the grief of seeing his only son dead, remembered the instructions of his master and knew it was his duty to take payment for all bodies. His wife, being a slave, was penniless, so Harichand told her she could pay with a piece of cloth. Lacking any other cloth, she was forced to tear her sari in two, thus unveiling herself. Just then, Visvamitra in his Brahmin disguise appeared at the pyre, and the virtuous queen, not wanting to show a strange man her unveiled face, hid in the hut reserved for wives about to commit suttee.

Left alone with Harichand, Visvamitra accused Hirali of being a cannibal and ordered Harichand to execute her summarily. Ever obedient, Harichand was just about to slay his wife when, with a trembling of the earth as Indra judged that Visvamitra had pushed Harichand far enough, the great god stayed his hand and admitted that Harichand could not be made to lose his virtue. Manikchand's body, which had not been consumed by the flames, was brought back to life and Harichand's kingdom and wealth were restored to him, so that he was able to buy himself, his wife and his son out of bondage and to resume his virtuous reign.

Raja Harichand's Punishment

Raja Harichand, a pious, wise ruler, showed his appreciation of divine mercy by giving one hundred pounds of gold everyday in alms to anyone in need who came to stand by his gate. One day decided to test Harichand's virtue descending to earth as a fakir and asking for alms. It was explained to him that next morning, when he would receive alms. But next day the strange fakir again arrived after the alms giving and was told to come back in the morning. On the third day, however. When the mendicant was again too late. Raja Harichand sent to ask what he wanted. Rani Bahal as his alms. At this the pious raja was outrages; but his wife, being learned in the scriptures, understood that he would not really have to give her to the fakir, only to give her in his thoughts. Still, however, Harichand refused.

God therefore sent two messengers to the raja to offer him a choice: he could have either twelve years of drought and famine throughout his kingdom or twelve hours of torrential rain, Now the raja reflected that his treasury and storehouses were full and could support the whole people for twelve years, whereas twelve hours of rain could wash away the entire kingdom; so he informed God's messengers that he chose the drought. Even as he spoke, however, all his servants and livestock turned to stone, while the gold and jewels in his treasury turned to charcoal. Only he and Rani Bahal were unchanged. Then the messengers told Harichand and Bahal that they would be unable to eat for three weeks, but would not die. However, they must seek a livelihood abroad, for the drought in their kingdom would not end until Shiva blew his horn there in twelve year's time.

Harichand and his rani therefore dressed

themselves as fakirs and set forth to live as best they might. On the second day they found a fruit tree in the jungle and thought to satisfy their hunger; but each time Harichand put out his hand the fruit moved away, and they had to walk hungrily on. On the fourth day they saw some fishermen at a fakir in the midst of a burning plain. For the first time in his life, Harichand went as a fakir to beg for starving wife, and received a fish. With it Harichand and Bahal walked on through the heat till they came to another tank near a town. Here the rani cleaned the fish and then sent her husband into the town to beg an earthen pot and some salt. When Harichand came back with a pot they kindled a fire and while the rani watched the pot Harichand went off to bathe. During his absence Bahal lifted the lid and to her amazement the fish jumped out of the pot into the tank and swam away. To spare him, Bahal told her husband on his return that her hunger after four days had been so great that she had eaten up all the fish herself. Harichand forgave her, and they wandered on. Some days later Harichand made a bow and arrow out of sticks in the jungle and shot two pigeons, which as before they prepared to eat. While they were cooking the rani left to bathe, and this time Harichand lifted the lid, whereupon the pigeons flew away. Now he realized what had happened to the fish, and they made no more attempt to find food.

On day Bahal remembered a wealthy oil merchant, who had always professed great friendship for them. Sure that he would be kind to them, they painfully walked to his home, which was far away. When they reached their friend's house, however, and he saw how far they had sunk, he showed them no respect or kindness, but gave them a wretched room to live in and such bad food that, hungry as they were, they could not attempt to it. So they left the oil merchant and wandered on for another week till they reached the kingdom of another friend, Raja Bhoj. Here they were well and kindly received. Platters of delicious food were began to crawl with maggots. On the first night, as Bahal lay sleepless with hunger, she saw a crack open in the wall, and into the crack disappeared the costly gold necklace which Raja Bhoj's daughter had left hanging there. Now Rani Bahal, who understood the ways of the supernatural, knew that if the wall were broken open the necklace would not be found, and that they would be accused of stealing it; so she woke Harichand and they stole out into the night. In the morning Raja Bhoj concluded that they were indeed thieves.

The unhappy couple wandered into another kingdom, which was also ruled by a friend, Raja Nal. But by now they were too ashamed to approach friends, and they knew that in two day's time the three weeks of starvation would be over. Harichand went into the jungle and brought enough back for sale in the bazaar to allow them to buy a little food. Thus after three weeks they praised God and ate.

Every day Harichand went to the jungle to collect grass and thus earned money to hire a hut in the bazaar and to buy just enough food to keep alive. After two years they had even saved enough to buy a scythe; now Harichand could bring far more grass to market, and with the profits Rani Bahal began to buy sils. With these she made exquisite horse trappings, an art known only to the high born and at which she was supremely skilful. When she had made four head collars. Bahal took them to Raja Nal's palace and sold them to his stables. As soon as Raja Nal saw the silk trappings he knew that they have been made by Rani Bahal and called the poor woman back; recognizing her, he asked her how she had sunk so low, to which she replied that it was God's will. Then Harichand was brought by Raja Nal's servants from the jungle where he was working. When he saw his old friend he repeated that their abasement was God's will. But Raja Nal gave them a palace to give in and servants. Thus they lived for four and a half years and no further ills befell them. Ten and a half years had now passed, and one day Shiva chanced to pass through Harichand's kingdom. All was brown and parched, for nothing could grow in the total drought. Nevertheless, to his surprise, Shiva saw farmers ploughing. He asked them why troubled to plough when surprise, Shiva saw farmers ploughing. He asked them why they troubled to plough when their efforts could never be rewarded. They replied that they practised their skills lest they forgot how to plough. Shiva reflected that this was a wise answer and that he himself might forget how to blow his horn. Therewith, he his horn and blew a mighty blast. This was the signal ordained by God to mark the end of the drought, and instantly rain began to fall.

Though only ten and a half years had passed, God was not displeased that the drought had been ended: he was happy for Shiva to do what pleased him. He therefore sent a dream to Rani Bahal, telling her and Harichand to return to their kingdom: and so they returned, to find prosperity and plenty restored. Soon afterwards they again visited their friend Raja Bhoj. They were given the same bedroom to sleep in as before, and that night the wall opened to reveal the missing necklace.

The Snake-Woman and King Ali Mardan

Ali Mardan Khan was Governor of Kashmir (not king) under Shah Jahan about 1650. A.D. This Himalayan province, already associated with the Hindu heavens, reached the height of its splendour under Mogul rule. In the previous generation Jehangir had added to the natural beauties of the mountains and the famous lake at Srinagar the man-made glories of the Shalimar gardens, a setting in which wonderful happenings occasioned no surprise. During Ali Mardan's well remembered and magnificent governorship, Shah Jahan ordered the construction of the Shalimar gardens at Lahore in imitation. The device of taking the form of a beautiful yet pathetic woman, bereft and weeping, in order to ensnare the hero is one often employed by rakshasis (female rakshasas, or ogres) in Indian legends. Snakes, like rakshasas, occupy an ambiguous role in Hindu folklore, a link between the malevolent and beneficent forces of nature-as they do in religion. They are associated with the deep-rooted cults of earth deities of the earliest inhabitants of India, just as the rakshasas are identified with those people themselves. It is thus highly inappropriate that a snake woman or Nagini should call herself a 'foreigner' to the Mogul ruler, who really was alien in India. Perhaps the legend should be regarded as a parable, demonstrating how the Hindu yogi protects the

Moslem overlord from the machinations of the more primitive Indians.

In Hinduism itself the snake has been incorporated in both the Shiva and the Vishnu cults. Though most snakes are personification of evil, a demon-killing cobra is one of the attributes of Shiva's fierce aspect, and Vishnu the Preserver floats on the cosmic ocean lying on the coils of a snake. With the help of a snake the gods acquired from the cosmic ocean the 'seven precious things', which included Vishnu's jewel Kaustubha. The connection between snakes, the ocean and jewels is therefore commonplace. The legend of Vikramaditya illustrates the notion of snakes as the guardians of underground treasure. The Nagas, snakes who rule the nether regions of Patala and have five or seven hoods, adorn them with the finest jewels in the universe. Like their guardians, these jewels may enthral men but, as Ali Mardan recognized, are best consigned to the water depths where they belong.

King Ali Mardan one day left his palace at Srinagar and went hunting in the forest which lay beyond the Dal lake. Deep in the forest he came upon a most beautiful girl sitting beneath a tree weeping. Immediately smitten with her charms, Ali Mardan asked her the cause of her grief. She told him she was the Emperor of China's hand maiden and had become lost while wandering in his pleasure gardens (which was a way of saying that she was a

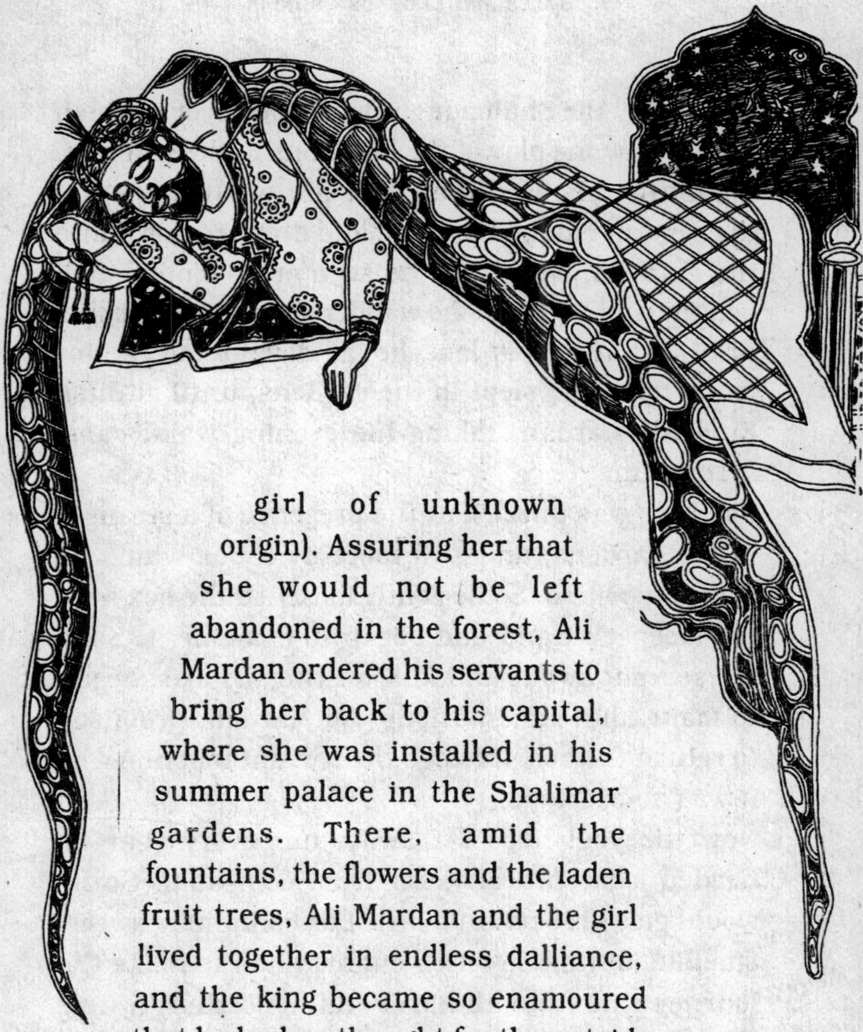

girl of unknown origin). Assuring her that she would not be left abandoned in the forest, Ali Mardan ordered his servants to bring her back to his capital, where she was installed in his summer palace in the Shalimar gardens. There, amid the fountains, the flowers and the laden fruit trees, Ali Mardan and the girl lived together in endless dalliance, and the king became so enamoured that he had no thought for the outside world or for his kingdom.

After some time, a yogi's servant, who had been sent by his master to fetch holy water from Lake Gangabal in northern Kashmir, was walking by the Shalimar gardens when over the high wall he saw the play of the fountains in the sunlight. Forgetting his errand at the sight of such beauty, the servant climbed the wall and dropped down into the gardens. Never had he seen or imagined such beauty, and for hours he wandered about marvelling until, exhausted at last, he lay down to sleep. For many hours he slept in the gardens, until at dusk King Ali Mardan, taking hie evening walk, came across him.

The king was puzzled at the presence of a stranger in his gardens, and still more by a box which he saw in his hand. So he gently loosened the box from the sleeper's hand and began to examine it. Soon the servant awoke and, discovering his loss, began to make loud lamentations. Ali Mardan, promised to return the box provided the servant told him why it was so precious.

Now the yogi lived far away, but every year he needed a jar full of water from Gangabal. So he would give his servant a little box containing sweet-smelling ointment which enabled him to make the journey safe from all harm and in so short a time that the yogi was never without the holy water. As soon as the servant told him of the ointment's properties, Ali Mardan realized that his master must be a very powerful yogi indeed, and resolved to summon him to his presence. He therefore told the servant to return to his master and inform him that

King Ali Mardan had the box and would not give it back until the yogi himself came to claim it.

The servant was forced to return to his master without the magical aid of the ointment, and the long journey took two and a half years. When he reached his master, the yogi was justly angry; but as Ali Mardan had foreseen, he was obliged to undertake the arduous journey to Srinagar. Thus five years passed, during which King Ali Mardan continued to live in the Shalimar palace with the beautiful girl; but despite his love, Ali Mardan could find no happiness.

At length the learned yogi arrived at his palace, and Ali Mardan received him with all due honour and respect, so that he forgot his anger. Seeing the king's drawn white face and glassy stare, he wished to help him, and asked if there were any strange woman in the palace. The king told him of the beautiful hand maiden of the Emperor of China. The yogi, however, with his supernatural insight, recognized by certain infallible signs that Ali Mardan was in thrall to the stranger. Without hesitation he assured the king that this beautiful girl was without doubt a snake-woman or Lamia. This was a snake over two hundred years old which had the power to turn itself into a woman. Despite his uneasiness the king could not at first be persuaded, for he still loved her; but at last he agreed to be guided by the yogi in testing the girl.

The king and his beloved always ate from the same dish, but one day Ali Mardan had one part of the food prepared with a great deal of salt and the other with sugar. Th evening he turned the salt side towards the girl; and she, seeing him eat his portion without complaint, ate hers too. That night, as Ali Mardan lay by her side feigning sleep, the girl became consumed with thirst. Now it was well known that if a Lamia wished to go at night she had to change back into her snake form. And so it was that the girl, thinking the king asleep and longing for a drink, transformed herself into a hideous and deadly snake and slithered out of the bedroom.

Ail Mardan, following her, saw the snake drink at every fountain in the Shalimar gardens until she reached Dal lake; there she bathed and drank till dawn, when she resumed her lovely human shape and slipped back into the palace.

Sorrowing and horrified, Ali Mardan asked the yogi how to rid himself of this creature. The yogi advised him to hide his suspicions and meanwhile to have a massive oven made of one hundred metals and with a padlocked door placed in the gardens and secured to the ground with heavy chains.

When all was prepared, Ali Mardan proposed that he and the girl should amuse themselves by cooking their own picnic in the gardens. Unsuspecting and full of gay laughter, the snake-woman agreed; so when the king had made bread, she took it from him and reached to put it in the oven. No sooner did she bend over than Ali Mardan pushed her in and locked the door. Then the king and the yogi piled fuel on the fire until the oven became white hot. The struggles and convulsions of the snake-woman continued for hour after hour within, and would have thrown the oven in the air had the chains not held it. At last, after a day and a night, all became still, and the oven was allowed to cool. When the door was opened a heap of ashes was all that remained, and among them a small stone. This, said the yogi, was the essence of the snake-woman, and anything it touched would turn to gold. But Ali Mardan, declaring that such a possession could only arouse greed and strife, threw the stone into the Indus, where it lies to this day.

Tales from Southern India

The Story of Atirupa

The kingdom of the Setupatis, whose capital was Madurai, formed part of the great southern empire of Chandragiri. Though a subject kingdom, Madurai had a distinguished history as capital of the Pandyas and as the great centre of Tamil culture. As the legend of Atirupa illustrates, Madurai attempted to reassert its influence from within the Chandragiri Empire. As in the legend, however, the city was subject to frequent attacks; these were partly attracted by the fabled jewels in the temple of Minakshi, Madurai's guardian deity and consort of Shiva.

In the kingdom of the Setupatis lived an astrologer named Satyavak. So renowned was his skill that people came from distant lands to consult him. But though he spent the greater part of his time in casting horoscopes and in giving advice and could have been handsomely paid, Satyavak remained poor, for he never accepted money for his services. Instead, he would beg for two hours a day, and would thus get barely enough to support himself and his wife.

One day his wife fell to thinking about this and wondering why he chose to remain in poverty. That evening she asked her husband, who replied that happiness could not be bought by money, and its acquisition corrupted, while their simple life protected them from such sins. He revealed that he had cast his own and his wife's horoscopes. He had thus learned that though they would have an only son in his sixtieth year, the son would not be of any service to them in their old age. Thus it was ordained that they should not attain happiness in this life; so the best way to use their present life was to obtain as much merit as possible.

In due course, as Satyavak had predicted, a son was born to them. He was a beautiful child, and they named him Atirupa. When he was five years old his father began to teach him: first a general education and then his special skills as an

astrologer. The child was an apt pupil; indeed by his sixteenth year, he had surpassed his father in learning and fame. The father was happy at this, for he was now old, but he continued to support his family by begging.

One day, while Satyavak was out begging, the

king of the Setupatis himself appeared at their little house. Atirupa explained that his father was out; but added that he saw from the king's face that some enemy had invaded his dominions and that the reason for this visit was to seek advice as to whether he should offer resistance. Explaining that the matter was urgent, for the enemy had entered the east gate of the city ten minutes before, Atirupa advised the king not to fight, for the stars were badly placed for him; instead he should seek shelter with his family in the jungle for three years. At the end of that period he would get back his kingdom without any direct attempt. At this moment a messenger arrived to announce the entry of the enemy by the east gate; but the king, hastening away, was able to save his family as Atirupa had advised. That evening, when Atirupa related all this to his father, the old man began to weep. At last he explained the cause of his unaccustomed emotion. He could not accept the destiny which had brought him such an accomplished son, who had been of such service to his sovereign at the age of sixteen; which yet had ordained that Atirupa should live only eighteen years — for this was the meaning of his enigmatic prediction to his wife. Atirupa's mother was overcome with grief at this news; and seeing his parents' unhappiness over him, the loving son made use of his great astrological knowledge. He asked his father for his horoscope, studied it for some time, and then by various false reasonings proved to his father that he had wrongly cast his horoscope, and that in fact he would live a hundred years. Thus by skilful argument Atirupa comforted his parents. But he himself had clearly seen how accurate his father's prediction had been.

Knowing he had only two more years to live, Atirupa began to wonder how, without arousing his parents' suspicions, he could make a pilgrimage to Benares to perform the prescribed religious rites for his parents — rites which only a son can perform for the souls of his parents. At last he decided that it would be better to go to Benares and die there than to remain at home where his parents would know of his death and might die of grief. If he disappeared from home without a word, they would at least be sustained by doubt and hope. Thus six months later he departed from home in the night and made his way north. As he travelled he left a trail of vague clues that he had gone on a pilgrimate for a few years; and his parents, following these, clung to the hope that one day he would return.

Meanwhile, Atirupa walked on, begging for food as he went. He dared not practise his astrologer's art for fear of giving away his identity. All went well for about two months, so long as he remained in regions which spoke his Tamil tongue. But when he reached the kingdom of Chandragiri, he found he could obtain nothing by begging, for the people did not understand him. Reaching Chandragiri city, he found a great pavilion bustling with preparations for a marriage. The chief minister's son was to be married in two days' time to the princess of Chandragiri. Atirupa discovered that the customary feeding of Brahmins at such festivities was to begin that evening. So while waiting for this he rested on the shadowy veranda of a nearby mansion.

Now the minister had shamefully deceived the king in arranging this match. He had been asked by the king to find a suitable husband for the princess, who was exceptionally beautiful and well educated. At once he offered to journey to the south to bring back information about the princes there. But instead of doing so, he hid himself for a while and then returned to the king with portraits of very ugly young men which he had painted out of his imagination but which he described as the Pandyan prince, the Chola prince, and so forth. The king would have none of these hideous men. So the minister pretended to go searching in the north; but produced another selection of deformed creatures. And so the king became convinced that no prince existed who was worthy of his daughter's hand and the succession to his empire. At this the minister produced a flattering portrait of his own son; and at once the king declared that this should be his daughter's husband, and fixed an early marriage date.

Now the minister's son was handsome, though not so handsome as he appeared in his father's portrait. But the minister had deceived the king even more grievously over his son than he had over the various princes; for the son was not only stupid and uneducated, he was also subject to violent epileptic fits on every alternate day, beginning early in the morning and lasting till evening. However, no one outside the minister's household knew of this. Nevertheless, for all his care and plotting, the minister's plans seemed about to founder; for the day set for the wedding would coincide with a day on which his son would be

incapacitated by a fit. At last the minister thought of a solution: he would find a substitute to go through the ceremonies, he would bribe the priests to acquiesce, and before the night came he would replace the substitute with his son, who by that hour would be restored to normal health. While pondering how he might find a substitute who was unknown in the city, was young and handsome, and would be at his mercy, the minister returned to his home and on the veranda stumbled over the sleeping Atirupa; for the house where he had sought refuge was the minister's own! Here was the perfect substitute, thought the minister, as he looked at Atirupa's fair features, which closely resembled the extravagant portrait he had given of his own son. He asked the boy in the Telugu tongue who he was, but received no reply. Then he tried Sanskrit, and Atirupa replied that he was a poor Brahmin, who needed money to continue his pilgrimage to Benares; more he would not tell. At once the minister told him his plan; and Atirupa, whose only wish was to perform the rites for his parents at Benares, agreed to be the substitute bridegroom and then to disappear from Chandragiri in return for the necessary money. He realized that having heard the minister's plans he was at his mercy, and if he did not agree would never reach Benares;

besides, as a married man he would be able to perform even more completely the proper rites for his parents.

Thus on his second day in Chandragiri Atirupa was dressed in a fine marriage costume, the decorations covering him from head to foot, so that only part of his face could he seen. With pomp Atirupa was conducted along the great pavilion which stretched between the minister's house and the palace, where the rites were to be performed. No one but the few priests whom the minister had bribed and threatened with their

lives could have recognized that this was not the minister's son. The princess, however, catching sight of his eyes, rejoiced that she was to be married to such a noble-looking and intelligent man. The ceremonies of the first day lasted long, with many rites and oblations to be performed by Atirupa. The day was drawing to a close when at last moment came for the formal completion of the marriage and Atirupa tied the cord about his bride's neck. Then, to the sound of music and drums, the remaining rites were hurriedly performed, for the auspicious hour for the couple's entry into the decorated hall where they would spend the night was near. No sooner was the last word of the last prayer said than the women of the household entered to conduct the pair to the bridal hall. At this, according to custom, all the men had to withdraw; so the minister had no time to substitute his son. Thus Atirupa found himself alone in the decorated hall with the princess; and as the queen had ceremonially locked the door to the hall, he had to remain.

Atirupa's thoughts were gloomy, for he felt sure the minister would not spare his life when he emerged next morning. He threw off his wedding garments and sat reflecting that now he might not live to perform the rites at Benares. The princess became anxious to see her husband so sad, and brought him the fruits and sweetmeats that had been provided for them. He tasted a little, then sang a song in Sanskrit. Though a learned lady, the princess did not understand the verse; so, gently, Atirupa expounded its meaning, ending after two hours of discourse in Sanskrit, during which the princess began to appreciate the nobility of her husband's thought, with the reflection: 'Sweetmeats to a hungry stomach are like beauty to unchaste women. Rice is the food I need to satisfy my hunger, as it is chastity which a woman needs to be called beautiful.' At once the princess humbly improvised a stove with the ceremonial dishes that had been left in the decorated hall, washed away the marriage spices from some rice and, lighting a fire with the scented sandalwood sticks placed about the room, cooked the rice in some milk and offered it to her husband. Atirupa found joy in the thought that his wife, even if she was to be his wife for a short time only, was such an intelligent, willing and resourceful lady. After he had eaten, they lay down to rest, but conversation in which each delightedly discovered the noble nature of the other kept them awake.

All too soon the dawn arrived and preparations for the second day's ceremonies began. At sunrise the anxious minister sent a palanquin to bring his 'son' back to his home. Though the fault was not his own, and he had at no point admitted to the princess that he was not the minister's son, he expected retribution. To Atirupa's surprise the minister had ready for him another palanquin loaded with three thousand gold mohurs; in this he was hurried away and borne swiftly to the borders of the Chandragiri empire. The minister's son meanwhile was dressed in the same marriage robes as Atirupa had been and joyfully conducted to the marriage hall for the remaining rites.

As the minister's son entered the hall, no suspicion was aroused; but the princess, eagerly seeking the intelligent eyes of her husband, with dismay encountered the lifeless gaze of the minister's son. Quickly she decided that if she revealed the deceit she might bring shame on her family and endanger the man whom she considered her real husband. She therefore said nothing and allowed the rites to proceed; in her heart, however, she swore to Shiva that she would perform the most extreme austerities in his honour if he would give her back her husband.

That night the bridal pair were once more locked into the decorated hall. But no sooner had the door been closed behind the minister's son, than the princess gave vent to her anger, demanding to know who he was. When he replied that he was her husband, the princess drew a sword; and at the sight of it the minister's son fell to the ground in an epileptic fit. Filled with repugnance for this pathetic creature, the princess called for the door to be unlocked: the minister's shame was revealed.

The third and final day of ceremonies had nevertheless to be completed. At their close the minister's son once more tried to enter the princess's chamber. She, heaping abuse on his head, forced him to tell her the true story. When he told her that the substitute was a poor Brahmin who was now continuing on his pilgrimage, she rejoiced that at least her true husband was still alive. Then she told the minister's son that he might pose as her husband to the outside world, but was never again to enter her presence. Of her real design to regain Atirupa she told no one.

The princess, who had formerly lived in luxury, now lived the life of a penitent, imposing on herself the most fearful austerities. Her parents worried at this change and begged her to tell them the reason, but she would tell them only that her penances would last

until she had attained her desires. Meanwhile she asked her father for money, and with it set up travellers' rest-houses at frequent intervals on the road from Chandragiri to Benares.

With the aid of the minister's money, Atirupa had soon reached Benares, where he piously performed the rites for his parents and for himself. Then, knowing that he had another year to live, he went on to Prayaga, where he continued his holy life and freely gave advice to all based on his astrological skill. As the appointed day of his death approached, Atirupa took to using unfrequented paths through the jungle when he went down to the Ganges to bathe, for he did not want his death to be observed. And one day, while returning along such a path, he slipped and fell down dead.

Now at the very moment of his death, the penances of the princess bore fruit. Shiva appeared to her and, having heard of her desire to regain her husband, promised that her wishes would be fulfilled. When he returned to his heaven, however, Shiva was informed by the sage Narada that the princess's husband had been granted only eighteen years of life and had died that very day. But Shiva could not break his promise to the princess, and did not wish her penances to go unrewarded; he therefore ordained that Atirupa should lie dead for three days, but on the fourth day be brought back to life.

Thus on the fourth day Atirupa came to life once more. Finding himself besmeared with mud, and remembering vaguely how he had fallen, he could not at first understand what had happened to him. But he knew that the day of his death had come and gone, and that he was still alive. At once he began to think of his aged parents and of the grief and loneliness they must be suffering, and he decided that he must return to them. Next morning, therefore, with a great vessel of Ganges water on his shoulder and dressed like any other poor pilgrim, Atirupa set off on the long journey home.

Now the very first rest-house at which Atirupa stopped happened to be one of the thousand and one set up on the pilgrims' route by the princess of Chandragiri. When he had been sumptuously entertained by one of the princess's officers and was about to continue on his journey, the officer handed him a palm leaf on which was inscribed a Sanskrit verse, and asked him whether he could interpret it. Atirupa looked at the verse, and to his astonishment, found it was the one he had recited to the princess on their wedding night. Saying that he understood it, but could not explain to the officer, Atirupa attempted to leave. But the officer fell at his feet and informed him that the rest of his journey was to be made in palanquin. Then he explained that the rest-house had been established by the princess of Chandragiri, who had ordered that each pilgrim should be shown the verse. The pilgrim who could understand it was to be conducted to her immediately. Atirupa was the first pilgrim of the thousands who had passed who had shown any knowledge of the verse. Rejoicing that his wife was trying to regain him, Atirupa stilled his fears of what the minister and his son might do to him in their fury, and entered the palanquin.

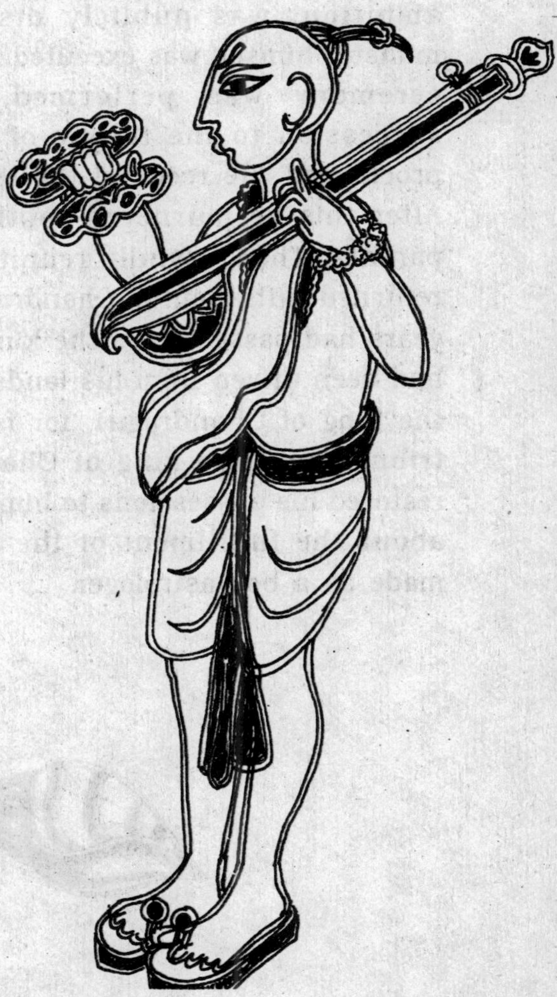

Soon he arrived at Chandragiri and, as a pilgrim bearing Ganges water, performed a public ceremony at the court. The princess, dressed once more in royal robes and stepping forward to help him, declared before the great assembly that this was her true husband. Then, calling for the arrest of the minister, she explained all. The minister's son, merely the instrument of his father's ambition, was publicly disgraced; but the minister himself was executed. A second wedding ceremony was performed, and Atirupa's succession to the throne of Chandragiri was proclaimed. He received the title Yuvaraja.

After this he journeyed south to seek out his parents. Then, joyfully reunited with them, he returned with them to Chandragiri. Exactly three years had passed since the king of the Setupatis had been driven from his lands by his over-lord, the king of Chandragiri, for failure to send his tribute; now, as king of Chandragiri, Atirupa restored his possessions to him and thus brought about the fulfillment of the prophecy he had made as a boy astrologer.

Ranavirasang

The legend of Ranavirasang is one of numerous southern tales centering on the efforts of a wicked minister to oust the rightful heir to the throne and to establish his own dynasty. The theme reflects the troubled history of the southern kingdoms and of courts where intrigue was always to be suspected. Vanjaimanagar is the classical name for the ancient city known as Karur, in the Cauvery valley in the state of Madras. In the legend, the princess of Cauvery is married to the person who succeeds in curing her of a fatal illness. A variant of this common theme appears in the Guru Gugga legend, though there the princess is cured on behalf of the suitor. It is just one of the ordeals put in the way of legendary heroes. These impossible tasks may be accomplished by brute force, with the aid of animals or spirits, by clever strategy, or by ruse — as exemplified by Raja Rasalu, the Boy with the Moon on his Forehead, and Hirde Shah. Hirde Shah's feats induce the Moslem princess to abase herself before him, and throughout the element of 'courtship display' is plain. The historical counterpart was the swayamvara, which was held for princesses to choose their bridegrooms where there were dynastic considerations, as described in the legend of the Jackal-mad.

In ancient times the city of Vanjaimanagar was ruled by a wise and just king called Sivachar. Prosperity reigned in his domains, but the king knew no peace in his heart for, having no son to perform his funerary rites, he expected to suffer the torments of hell. He also knew that his minister, an evil tyrant called Kharavadana, rejoiced at his misfortune, for he hoped to seize the throne for his own family after the king's death. The goof king did not lose hope, but continued to offer every sort of sacrifice to the gods and to perform every work of charity. At last in his sixtieth year his prayers were answered and a son was born to him.

This son, Sundara, was brought up with every care under the guidance of Sivachar's faithful steward Ranavirasang. When the boy was only ten, however, Sivachar felt the approach of death and, calling Ranavirasang to him, placed Sundara in his care. Sivachar was well aware that Kharavadana would take every opportunity of his position as regent during Sundara's minority to advance his own fortunes; so he strictly enjoined Ranavirasang to guard the boy against the minister's machinations and if necessary to save his life rather than attempt to retain the kingdom for him. Then the king sent for Kharavadana and, handing him his signet ring, entrusted the regency of the kingdom to him until Sundara was sixteen, and asked him to find a suitable wife for him. And with these words the king died.

Kharavadana then assumed the government of the kingdom, while Sundara remained in the palace under the care of Ranavirasang. Faithful to his promise to the dead king, Ranavirasang kept close watch on the prince, never letting him out of his company. Nothing in the prince's education was neglected, and tutors in every branch of knowledge were brought to the palace, where Sundara shared his lessons with twenty other boys of good family. These became Sundara's constant companions. In due course the minister provided a bride for the prince; but though Ranavirasang could not forbid the marriage, he would not allow the two to live together as man and wife, nor ever to

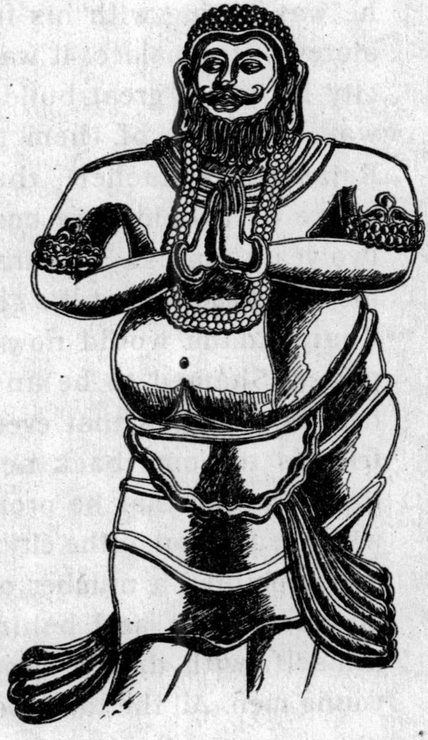

be alone together. Sundara was not allowed at any time to leave the palace and soon became bored and discontented. He could not understand why his guardian so hedged him in; for Ranavirasang had not wished to alarm his charge by telling him that Kharavadana had offered a huge reward to anyone who succeeded in assassinating the prince. Sundara's sixteenth year came, but nothing was said by the minister of his assuming power in his own right; nor did Ranavirasang raise the matter.

One day, when Sundara was already eighteen, he was sitting with his friends on the seventh storey of the palace. It was dusk and across the city he saw a great building. He asked what it was, and one of them told him that it was Rajasthanik Kacheri, the seat of government where he should have been sitting for the past two years. And so Sundara learnt of the price on his own head and of the general assumption that Kharavadana would now never relinquish his power. Shamed to be an object of pity of his friends, Sundara that evening asked his twenty friends to come back next day and informed Ranavirasang that he proposed to go out riding with them through the city. Ranavirasang agreed, but appointed a number of horsemen to ride as guards before and behind the party and he himself, with drawn sword, accompanied the young men. All the townspeople paid due homage to their old king's son; but when they passed the minister's mansion Kharaviradana ostentatiously failed to salute the prince.

That night in his bedroom, when Ranavirasang had left him alone for a few minutes, Sundara noticed a rope ladder in the corner of the room. Hardly pausing to think, he used it to make his escape from the palace which seemed a prison-house. It was a new-moon night and dark; but until the city settled for the night, Sundara decided to hide behind a nearby house. While waiting he heard a conversation inside between a Brahmin and his wife. The Brahmin said that he had been waiting in vain for the prince's majority: plainly he would never gain power. Meanwhile the city was governed by a tyrant and a good man could no longer bear to live in the degenerate city. Next day they would leave for ever. Sundara's pride again received a heavy blow and he resolved to risk his life to win back his kingdom.

When all was still, he wandered on. It began to rain, and Sundara sought shelter in a temple of Ganesa. Hardly had he entered it than two shepherds followed him. Sundara hid in the shadows and overheard one of the shepherds interpreting the chirps of some lizards in the temple. The shepherd explained that they were saying that the son of their beloved king Sivachar was now in the temple. Then the lizards chirped again: the minister and his secretary were coming to that very temple for a secret meeting, explained the shepherd. At that moment a carriage was heard and the shepherds fled. Sundara, now appreciating Ranavirasang's wisdom, hid and held his breath behind the image of Ganesa. At once Kharavadana and his secretary entered. The minister vented his fury that Sundara had been able to ride about the city unharmed and free: why had none of his servants obeyed the orders to kill the prince? The secretary began by suggesting that Sundara was harmless, for he made no demands; but seeing the look on the minister's face, he promised that he himself would kill the prince before another week was out. Their discussion ended, the minister and his secretary re-entered their carriage and prepared to drive away. Sundara, meanwhile, summoning his courage, decided to risk all to discover more of their plots, and silently climbed on to the back of their carriage.

A long drive brought them to a park beyond the west side of the city in the middle of which was a large, brightly lit tank. Before they reached the lights Sundara dropped off and hid behind some trees to observe what would happen. The carriage drove along a causeway planted with flowering trees to the centre of the tank where, at a richly decorated, flower-filled summer house twenty beautiful girls welcomed the minister. Sitting on a golden couch, Kharavadana asked them to bring the queen. While ten went off with a palanquin to bring her, Sundara waited eagerly to see what woman could overshadow these in beauty. The palanquin arrived, the queen stepped out, and Sundara recognized — his wife! At once she began to chide

the minister for not having taken the opportunity of the morning's ride to rid her of her husband. He offered his excuses and promised swift death for Sundara, and they retired to bed. Just then an owl could be heard hooting. Now one of Kharavadana's maids could understand the hootings of owls and, eager to earn the promised reward, informed the minister that the hootings told her the prince was lurking behind one of the trees in the park. Seizing torches, all the maid-servants and the minister himself began to search to park. But Sundara was too quick for them: flying like a kite, he jumped over a wall and soon was in the north part of the city. By now, however, word of his escape had spread, and greedy hands sought him in every street. Sundara took refuge in an almshouse built by his father and lay down among the beggars sleeping there.

Living in a cave outside the North Gate of the city was a gentleman robber. He was very fastidious about what he would steal, rejecting gold and silver as beneath contempt and picking only certain precious jewels; also, he robbed only once every seven years. He always used a coolie to carry the booty, killing him afterwards. This night happened to be the appointed night for his raid; and as he had heard the prince was abroad, he decided to rob the palace. Just as Sundara was falling into an exhausted sleep in the almshouse, the robber entered and chose him as his coolie. Sundara could see nothing in the dark, but the robber rubbed his eyes with a sort of kohl, and this enabled him to see clearly but himself to remain invisible. Thus Sundara helped to rob his own palace, watching with amazement as the robber opened every lock by applying a leaf to it. Soon they had extracted all the precious stones and had escaped from the palace.

During this time the robber had been observing Sundara, without suspecting his real identity, and thinking he might make a fine husband for his beautiful daughter. With this thought, he secured Sundara in a cave cell whose entrance was covered by a huge boulder which opened and closed when he pronounced a magic incantation. Then he went to announce his intentions to his wife and daughter. His wife, however, advised him to do as usual and kill his coolie, and the robber agreed to give in to her wishes. But the daughter, once her father had expressed his first wish, felt herself to be Sundara's promised wife; her obligations now lay to her husband, and she secretly ran to the cave, pronounced the magic words to open it, and urged Sundara to flee, explaining her reasons for helping him, and begging him ultimately to marry her.

By now it was near dawn and the hunt for the prince had been abandoned. Sundara ran through street after street. At last he thought it safe to return to the palace. First, however, he paused near the doorstep of a Brahmin's house to regain his breath. While he rested, he heard the Brahmim foretell that the prince would be bitten to death within the hour by a black snake; the only thing that could save him would be a special sacrifice which would tie the mouth of the snake. The Brahmin's wife begged him to perform this sacrifice: but he explained that without ghee (clarfied butter) it could not be performed, and they had no money at all to buy ghee. At this Sundara, describing himself as a loyal herdsman of the palace, offered the Brahmin his ring to pawn. Money was thus obtained and the sacrifice performed just in time. Sundara now returned to the palace and to Ranavirasang. Explaining all and expressing his gratitude for Ranavirasang's previous caution, Sundara ordered the seizure of Kharavasang's and his shameless wife, of the maid-servants and of the robber and his wife; and summoned to the palace all those who had helped him during his night of peril, including the robber's daughter, whom he married. Then, having won his kingdom in one stroke, he reigned happily and well in Vanjaimanagar, relying on the wise advice of the faithful Ranavirasang.

Virtue Alone Conquers

Though this legend is cast as a didactic tale to prove that the gods always intervene to restore the balance of good and evil, it is based on real places and kingdoms in Madras. Tevai is the classical name of Ramnad or Ramanthapuram in the peninsula jutting out towards Ceylon, while the kingdom acquired by the prince through marriage is farther north, in the valley of the Cauvery.

In the city of the Tevai ruled a king called Suguan, whose excellent minister was called Dharmasila. The king's son Subuddhi and the minister's son Durbuddhi were the same age and, having been brought up and educated together, had become inseparable friends. Nevertheless their characters differed dramatically: the prince had a noble and generous spirit and had a motto 'Virtue alone conquers'; the minister's son, on the other hand, was mean and unfriendly to all and claimed as his motto 'Evil alone conquers'.

One day when they were still young boys, Durhuddhi spoke to his friend of his fears for the future; while the prince would one day be king and would marry a fine wife, he himself was doomed to become an outcast, for he was too much hated ever to become a minister or to find a wife. The prince assured him that he would always remain his friend and would appoint him minister. Then Durbuddhi asked him to promise that when he was married he would allow him to spend one night with his wife. The prince was taken aback at this request, but at his tender years hardly knew what it might mean and agreed, to please his friend.

Some years passed, and one day Subuddhi and Durbuddhi together with a party of friends went into the jungle to hunt. But the two friends, thoughtlessly pursuing a deer, became separated from the rest of the party and soon were lost. For hours they tried to find their way, but with no success. At last, hungry and nearly dying of thirst, they gave their horses their heads, and after several hours, long after nightfall, by which time both were in a state of collapse, the horses brought them to a large tank. As usual, before drinking the prince pronounced his motto; to his horror, he heard the answering motto, 'Evil alone conquers'. He chided his friend for uttering such an impiety when they had every cause to be grateful to providence for saving their lives, and urged him to mend his ways. At this Durbuddhi flew into a rage and fell upon the unsuspecting prince, beating him mercilessly and then tearing out his eyes and pushing sand into the sockets. Then Durbuddhi ran away with both horses, leaving Subuddhi for dead.

But life still remained, and at dawn Subuddhi found the strength to crawl about. Reaching the far side of the tank, he found by touch the entrance to a temple, which he entered, locking the gate behind him. Now this happened to be a temple of fierce Kalí, who had left it some time before. When she returned to find herself shut out of her own temple, she loudly threatened destruction to the usurper. Subuddhi, daring all for he knew that his wounds might kill him, refused to let her in unless she restored his eyes; and Kali, who could not otherwise

regain her temple, immediately restored his sight. Subuddhi opened the gates and vowed to remain Kali's servant for ever.

After some time Kali tried to persuade Subuddhi to return home; but he refused, hurt that his father had sent no seachers after him. He did not know that the minister, disbelieving Durbuddhi's story when he returned to Tevai, had banished him until he brought back the prince, thinking that this would ensure Subuddhi's return; but Durbuddhi had taken to wandering from city to city, not daring to enter the jungle or Tevai.

Some months later Kali, wishing to reward her servant, told him of the princess of Cauvery, whom she had afflicted with smallpox and then with blindness to punish her father for lapses in his customary devotion to her. The king had promised his daughter in marriage to whoever could cure her. Kali told Subuddhi to attempt the cure; and promised that with her aid the princess would regain her sight. And so it came to pass that Subuddhi cured the princess and became her husband. When the king of Cauvery learnt that the stranger was of royal blood his joy knew no bounds. The old man decided that he should hand over the reins of government immediately to this royal son-in-law. So Subuddhi found a wife and a kingdom. But in deference to the old king he continued to consult him on all matters and acted in every way respectfully to him.

One day, after several years had passed, Subuddhi chanced to look from the palace window and saw a familiar figure; the face had become as dark as a coolie's and the clothes were ragged, but there was no doubt that it was Durbuddhi. His good nature as strong as ever and moved by the pitiable condition of his old friend, Subuddhi at once forgave him. He brought him into the palace, fed him and clothed him. He told his wife and her family all about their lifelong friendship and of how they had been lost in the jungle; but of Durbuddhi's attempt on his life he said nothing. Thus Durbuddhi became accepted in the palace and, true to his promise, Subuddhi made his old friend his minister.

After some time he even used to send Durbuddhi every day to see the old king and present papers for signing. This gave the still wicked Durbuddhi the opportunity to wheedle his way into the king's confidence. After some tantalizing hesitation, he told the king that Subuddhi was not really of royal blood: that was why he had fled his native country. He was the illegitimate son of the king, from whom he inherited hie noble looks, and a barber woman, from whom he gained his medical skill. The king, overcome at the news that he had married his daughter and handed his kingdom to the son of a woman of one of the lowest castes, decided that the only way to expunge the dishonour of his family would be to kill both daughter and son-in-law. He ordered their execution.

Durbuddhi, learning of this, wished to take his last opportunity to keep his friend to the promise made when they were children that he could spend one night with his wife. Subuddhi, trapped by his promise, informed his wife that night she should admit Durbuddhi to her bedroom. Aghast at this order, the princess arranged with her mother's help for her foster sister to take her place. But unknown to Durbuddhi the king had ordered the execution for that very night. So it happened that the executioner, entering in the dark, beheaded the foster sister and Durbuddhi, who thus in contradiction of his motto fell victim to his own greatest evil.

GLOSSARY

Apsara	One of the water nymphs and dancers in Indra's heaven, a fairy.
Aryans	People who conquered northern India during the second millennium B.C.
Brahma	One of the three great gods of Hinduism, the Creator.
Brahmin	Member of the first of the four castes, many of whom are priests. Their semi-divine attributes stem from their knowledge of the Vedas.
Chaupur	A game of chance played with dice and with pieces on a cross-shaped board.
Devi	The Great Mother, consort of Shiva.
Darbar	Assembly of princes at the court of their overlord.
Dravidians	People considered the indigenous inhabitants of the Deccan, though they were probably themselves invaders in prehistoric times, who ousted those whose descendants are now the hill tribes.
Fakir	A religious mendicant.

Gram	Chick-peas.
Guru	A spiritual teacher.
Indra	Chief of the lesser gods.
Jinns	Demons with supernatural powers in Moslem tradition. Their Hindu equivalents are the rakshasas and yakshas.
Kali	Fierce form of Devi.
Kohl	Power used to darken the eyelids.
Kshatriya	Memeber of the second Hindu caste: the warrior caste to which kings belong.
Mahout	Elephant driver.
Moguls	A race, erroneously thought to be Mongol, but in fact of mainly Turkish origin, who conquered northern India in the sixteenth century.
Myna bird	Bird related to the starling which can be taught to speak, and on that account held sacred.
Palanquin	Covered litter for one person, carried by four or six bearers.

Pathans	Afghan troops of the Moguls.
Raja, rani	King, queen.
Rakshasa	Demon. (fem.**rakshasi**)
Rishi	Holy man or sage with superhuman powers. The Seven Rishis were the sons of Brahma.
Sari	Woman's costume, consisting of a length of cloth wrapped round the body, the end forming a head-covering and veil.
Shiva	One of the three great gods of Hinduism, the Destroyer.
Sipahi (sepoy)	Armed guard, soldier, or messenger.
Suttee	Burning of a Hindu widow on her husband's funeral pyre.
Swayamvara	Public assembly of suitors at which a princess chooses her husband.
Tank	Artificial pool, often ornamental and in the precincts of a temple, with steps leading down to it to allow ritual bathing.

Untouchable Non-caste person.

Vishnu One of the three great gods of Hinduism, the Preserver.

Vizir Chief minister.

Yogi Man who practises yoga, a system of mediatation and austerities whereby he seeks detachment and may achieve great physical powers. Some live by singing religious songs. Those who live by begging wear heavy earrings.